Praise for *Sensible & Sensational*
by Jenni James

"This book, like the rest in the series, is a straight-forward, modern-day telling of Austen's book. Jenni James is always fun and really gives the characters in this story their own voices. I love that the main character, Ellyn, has high-functioning autism. The author takes us into her mind and shows us what makes sense and doesn't, what is a challenge to her and how she deals with it. Everyone that sees the world through autism is different, but I love how seeing this story through Ellyn's eyes sheds light on this corner of the spectrum. I love books that bring awareness to ASD."
  —Happy Valley Book Reviews

"I love this writer so much. I have to be careful of when I start one of her books because I have no self-control and can't stop reading until it is done. They are clean and have wonderful character development. This book was fascinating to see the world through someone with autism's eyes. Yet again, well done, Jenni James."
  —Rachel Nagy, Amazon book reviews

"Wonderful. Absolutely one of the best books I've read. Jenni James has a way with words. She grabs your attention from the very beginning. Funny and cute and very clean romance. Zane cuddle therapy. Try it for yourself."
  —Jennifer R. Peel, Amazon book reviews

The Jane Austen Diaries

The Jane Austen Diaries
SENSIBLE & SENSATIONAL

The Jane Austen Diaries
SENSIBLE & SENSATIONAL

BY

JENNI JAMES

TRIFECTA BOOKS

This is a work of fiction, and the views expressed herein are the sole responsibility of the author. Likewise, characters, places, and incidents are either the product of the author's imagination or are represented fictitiously, and any resemblance to actual persons, living or dead, or actual events or locales, is entirely coincidental.

Sensible & Sensational

Book design and layout copyright © 2015 by Trifecta Publishing
Front cover design © 2015 by Jenni James

ISBN-978-0-9966246-1-9

Printed in the United States of America
Year of first printing: 2015

This book is dedicated to my son with autism.
You are my hero, my genius, and my light.

I love you.

ACKNOWLEDGMENTS

I would like to thank my Heavenly Father for the insight to produce a book with such a fascinating and gentle main character.

And I would like to thank my husband and kids, whose patience with me while I pursue my dream of writing so many books is the best. I love you all!

My dad died *suddenly six weeks ago, and my whole world crashed. I'd heard of pain before—that horrendous grieving pain that others talk about or you see in movies—but I'd never experienced it until then. I didn't realize how much I needed my dad until he was gone, either. At seventeen, I don't think you notice as much as you'd like to. Whatever it was, I didn't know how much I loved my dad until I couldn't tell him anymore.*

ONE

♥

SCHOOL BLUES

I hated going to new schools. I hated it. Like, seriously. Even that simple change from elementary to middle school and then to high school—it completely freaked me out. But this was worse. This was way way way way way... okay, so it was bad. Not only was it a new school in Bloomfield, New Mexico, but it was a new house—new city, new state—new school. As in, totally awkwardly confusing and chaotic and everybody in your face and talking at once and just—argh!! Why can't change happen without all the confusion?

"Hey, you're the new girl, right? Ellyn? Or are you the other twin, Maralyn?"

There, standing in front of me, was a very good-looking guy. Like, the total swim team/soccer nut athletic-type guy. And he was smiling this gorgeous smile while talking in this deepish voice, and . . . and . . . and . . . I blinked. "I'm sorry. What, um, what did you say?" *Stay cool, Ellyn. Take a deep breath and focus. Don't stress out. He's not too close. Just focus.*

The guy glanced down the hall—thankfully, it was beginning to thin out and wasn't so claustrophobic—and then he looked back at me and chuckled. Hazel eyes, all sparkly and—good grief! I was beginning to think like my sister Maralyn.

"Let's start at the beginning. Hi, I'm Zane."

Oh! He was holding out his hand. I switched my books and shook his hand. Maybe it was a little too hard—I didn't know. I really try to stay away from the whole touching thing, and have never quite mastered the art of—you know, shaking hands. "Hi. I'm Ellyn. But you can call me Ellyn, or um, Elly, or Ella, or even Elle. Or my mom calls me by my middle name and I really don't want to tell you what that is, so I won't." *Oh, my gosh. Can I be any more of a dork? Seriously?* I wanted to die. Why wasn't my sister there? She loves guys. Cute ones with gorgeous smiles, too. And she doesn't sound lame while trying to interact.

He laughed. "Well, what *do* you like to be called, then?"

I thought about it for a minute. No one had ever asked me that question before. "I don't know. I'm not sure."

His eyebrows rose.

I was probably scaring him. My shoulder twitched, and my throat went dry, and suddenly, my arm itched. I held on to my books tightly. *Do not scratch. Do not scratch.*

"Right. Well, I'll just call you Ellyn until you figure it out." He cleared his throat. "So, hi. I'm your guide for the day to kind of help you get to your classes."

What? I needed a guide? Was he serious? "Why?"

He seemed a bit hesitant. "The school assigned me to show you the ropes. You know, so things don't feel awkward for you."

He was going to be with me all day? *That* would be

awkward. I really, really wanted to be on my own. This wasn't good at all. "Okay. Thanks." I scratched my arm.

"So, who do you have first hour? Let's get you there."

"Oh. I remembered a few seconds ago, but now I forgot. I do that sometimes—just forget things." I switched my books to my other arm, reached into my back pocket, and pulled out my schedule.

"Yeah, I think we all forget stuff."

I nodded and attempted to unfold the paper one-handed. "Well, I'm particularly forgetful. I'm probably the queen of forgetfulness. I mean—not always. I'm really good at focusing until someone distracts me, or talks to me, or does something like stands next to me and breathes—yeah, then I just forget what I'm doing."

"Here. Let me help you before you drop one of those books." Zane gently took the paper from my hand.

I shifted the pile again. "My other school had an iPad, and all our curriculum was on it. It was nice. We didn't need to lug books around."

"It looks like you've got Mrs. Cheswick." He glanced down at the books I was carrying. "Would you like me to take some of those for you?"

"No, I'm good. They're no big—"

He took them anyway. "These are nothing. This is just the info from the school. Wait until you see the real books."

"What? Are you kidding me?" I could feel my chest tighten.

"Nope." His eyes twinkled as they looked down at me.

A small part of me began to panic. "Darn, I really hoped you were. I don't think I could carry anything else right now. And I also wish I had a backpack."

He nudged my shoulder and totally caused me to jump. "Hey, I was teasing. There aren't more books. We're not cool enough for iPads, but we've got laptops. And during flex period, I'll take you over and sign you up for one. Did you bring the thirty-five-dollar insurance fee for it?" He began to walk down the hall.

I followed him. "I don't know. Maybe." There was a fee? No one had told me about a fee. What happened if I didn't have the money that day? I wasn't even sure my mom had any extra cash right now—especially with losing Dad and just moving and now Maralyn and I would both need thirty-five dollars. Great.

"You think about stuff a lot don't you?"

I looked up to see those hazel eyes again. "You noticed, huh?" I tried not to wince as I glanced away. I wasn't sure I succeeded.

He shrugged. "I notice a lot of things. But don't worry—you're cute when you think."

"What?" My jaw dropped. No one had ever said anything like that to me before.

He stopped at a door. "Here we are. Your first class. Come on in." He stood back to let me pass.

I didn't budge. "What did you say?"

Zane grinned. "You heard me. Now come into your class."

I blushed. For no reason at all, this huge, awful flush came over me. "Okay." Clutching my elbows, I walked into the room and willed myself to calm down. The teacher looked over and stopped talking as I entered.

"Hello," she said.

All at once, a bunch of teens were staring at me and my red face. I blinked. Why did everyone have to stare? I hated it when I was the center of attention. *Please look away.* I could feel every single pair of eyes as if they were drills boring into me. It was too much. Too fast. Everything was a whirlwind of confusion, and I couldn't think. I couldn't do this right now.

Get out of here. Go. Run. Move. Now!

Just as Zane was closing the door, I bumped into him and pushed it back open again. As soon as I got into the empty hallway, I could feel my hands begin to shake and my heart race, and that stupid red face of mine only getting redder.

I was a freak. Everyone was going to think I was stupid for running out of class like that. Ugh.

"Hey, are you all right?"

Zane touched my shoulder. I quickly moved out of his reach, making sure my back was to him. "Yeah, I'm awesome. I just need a minute to myself first."

"That's cool. Take some time to relax. It's rough going to a new school, isn't it?"

Why was he talking? I didn't need more chatter right now—I needed calm. I took a deep breath and closed my eyes. I hated going to a new school. I hated it. Dad used to make it a little better for me. He always had a chocolate cake with sprinkles waiting for me and my sister when we came home. We all pretended it was a special occasion because it was a new school, but I knew it was because of me. Because this was the hardest part of being me. This right here. I just lost it sometimes and did weird things like run away.

Dad used to sneak me an extra piece of cake once everyone had left the kitchen. He'd hug me tight and tell me how proud he was of me and then ask way too many questions, which drove me nuts, but I needed them. I needed him. He made me feel normal and pretty and fun and … I missed him. I missed him so much.

"Ellyn?"

I didn't realize I'd started to cry until Zane handed me a tissue. It was crumpled, and he looked totally embarrassed.

"Sorry. It's not used—I swear! I put it in my pocket this morning. I promise."

I wasn't going to take it. I had this thing about crumpled tissues. But his face was adorable, and I didn't want to hurt his feelings, so I did. "Thank you."

"You're really shy, aren't you?" He grinned. I could tell he was still trying to figure me out.

I shook my head. "No. Not even close. I don't mind sharing—I just *can't* sometimes. I like people and learning and seeing new things, but I get overwhelmed if it's too much. My brain works faster than I can keep up with sometimes, and I tend to freak out a little bit until I can calm down and fix things one at a time."

I was worried that I might've scared him, but he seemed pretty chill about everything. He was probably supposed to be super nice to everyone, which is why the school chose him, because he was most likely the nicest guy here—but whatever the reason, I kinda liked feeling okay.

"So, do you have ADHD or something?" he asked, not in a mocking tone, just a matter-of-fact friendly chat-type tone, as if he were genuinely interested.

"No. Uh, it's different than that." I looked away.

"Would you like to tell me about it?"

I let the question hang between us. I was beginning to sort of like him. I mean, I wasn't dumb enough to believe we'd ever go out on a date or anything, but maybe we'd be friends or something. Except I knew that what I was going to say next would ruin it completely. Not that it mattered—I preferred to be on my own anyway. Maralyn was more the outgoing, popular type. I thought of myself as the nerdish, practical sister who sometimes sort of had episodes when things began to get crazy around me.

"Uh, yeah." I took a deep breath, twisted my hands together, and then sealed my fate. "I have high-functioning autism."

His face lit up, and he said the last thing I'd ever expected to hear from a teenager, the exact thing my dad had always said to me. "Oh, wow! So you're a genius."

TWO
♥
AN AWAKENING

By the end of school, I realized it probably hadn't been that bad of a day after all. Sure, there was definitely some awkwardness, but I think I did okay. The kids were friendly, so that was good too. And apart from stumbling over a few words, I survived Zane, which had to be some sort of record for me. Interacting with guys wasn't exactly my specialty. Okay, so I'd never really tried before. Or rather, there'd never really been a guy who'd wanted to get to know me. I honestly had no idea if Zane would ever talk to me again, now that I didn't need his help, but today had been a good day. He made me feel sort of normal. And I liked it.

Clutching my laptop and those darn books, I met up with Maralyn at the front of the school. "How'd it go?" I asked as she approached, looking like a model for a magazine ad.

She had all her things tucked nicely in a cute bag, and she grinned as she bounded toward me. We only had one class together—biology. We didn't even have the same lunch.

"Oh, my gosh, can you believe how awesome this school is? I'm going to love it here! There are so many fun boys." She held up a paper. "And I've already been asked to audition for the dance team!"

It figured she'd fit right in. I rolled my eyes, even though I was happy for her. "So it was that good, huh?"

She waggled her brows and grinned. "You have no idea. Plus, I've got a few digits of potential boys to date in my cell phone now." She held it out to show me.

"Ellyn! Wait up!"

We both glanced back, and I was sort of shocked to see Zane heading toward us. My heart jolted when he came up to us and smiled. "So, do you guys live over there?" He pointed the way we were headed.

"Yeah." Maralyn grinned and twirled her hair around her finger. She was totally checking him out. "Hi. I'm—"

"Maralyn. Yeah, I know. Hi. Welcome to the school. I'm Zane Ferrars." He turned to me. "So, Ellyn, could I join you? I'd be happy to walk you home."

Maralyn's jaw dropped.

I laughed, but I was more amazed than anything. No one ever ignored Maralyn. "Haven't you gotten sick of me yet?"

He slowly grinned and shook his head. His eyes looked bright green in the sunlight. "Are you kidding me? I've been dying to finish our debate."

"Wait." Maralyn looked at each of us. "You had a debate?"

I didn't know how to say this without hurting her feelings, but there's no way she would've been able to keep up with our conversation earlier. "Yeah, during lunch. He was trying to tell me that Nikola Telsa's technology was more advanced than Thomas Edison's, and I don't know if I'm buying it."

He looked surprised. "How could you not? The man invented wireless electricity, wireless lightbulbs in the eighteen hundreds. Can you imagine if he'd gotten his patent and we had those things now? None of us would have to be on the grid. I bet the technology would've advanced, and everything would be wireless. And I mean everything. Our TVs, computers, appliances, vacuums—you name it."

"Right." Maralyn chuckled and shook her head like we were crazy. "You two rocket scientists have at it. I'm gonna call my bestie from Arizona and see what she's doing." She flipped around and started walking home.

Dang it. She'd left me alone. All of a sudden, my throat went dry, and my arm started to itch again. Everything was different now. Zane's assignment was finished. He didn't *have* to be with me—now he *wanted* to hang out. "So, hi," I said, and then cleared my throat.

Zane's smile was contagious as he looked away and then back at me again. "Hi. So, did I interrupt something? Would you rather walk with your sister? Um ... I hope she's not mad."

"Yes. Well, no. I don't know." I was making no sense at all. I took a deep breath and tried again. "I'm sure she's fine. So, where do you live?"

"Probably right past you. Did you move into the house on Sycamore Avenue? The one that was for rent?"

"Yep." I wasn't sure if I should be worried or flattered that he knew where I lived.

"I thought so. I saw a moving truck the other day. I would've come over to help, but my dad needed me to work at his store. I don't mind the money, but man, I really don't like working there. Did you ever have a job like that?"

There was way too much information hitting me at once. I took another deep breath and tried to process. "So, you were going to come over and help us move in, but couldn't?"

"Sorry. Lame, I know."

I started to walk forward. "You really are nice. Who'd do that?"

He hitched his backpack on his shoulder and shrugged as he joined me. "Lots of people around here help each other. We're a smaller community, so we're used to being there for our neighbors."

I nodded, not sure what to think of people helping so much. It definitely sounded different.

"Where did you move from? I guess I never asked that earlier. Your sister's calling someone in Arizona. Is that where you lived? And what jobs have you had?"

I was imagining what it would have been to meet him the day we moved here. I heard him, but I honestly had no idea what he'd just asked me. So I pointed that out. "You really ask a lot of questions at once."

"I know. I'm probably confusing you, huh? I'll try not to."

"Not confusing—it's just that my brain sort of gets stuck on thinking about the first question, so I lose track and get overwhelmed if you keep asking more."

"Right. So let's start again. Where did you move from?"

Oh, so that's what he'd asked. "Chandler, Arizona."

"Okay. And where's that?"

"By Phoenix."

"Cool." He stopped to wait for a car to go by before we crossed the road. "What brings you here?"

Because my world ended when I lost my dad, my best friend. Because Mom couldn't afford to live in our big house anymore. Because she needed a job now that Dad was gone.

And when she got a job in Farmington, she couldn't afford the houses there, so we moved here, the next cheapest city. Because life seriously stinks and awful things happen and … "My dad died." I walked across the street. I felt a hollow feeling in my heart, and tried to stop it from forming into the hole I knew it'd become.

He quickly followed. "Whoa, Ellyn, I'm so sorry. Are you okay?"

Was he really asking me something that personal? "No. I'm not."

Putting his hands into his pockets, he waited a moment and then said softly, "When did it happen?"

My arm itched again. This time it was my elbow. It was really beginning to bug me. All at once, I wanted to be as far away from him as I could get, but it wasn't him. It was just the subject of the conversation. "If you're going to keep walking with me, could we talk about something else, please?"

He paused. "Uh, are you asking me to leave?"

"What?" I glanced over. Why would he think that? "No. I'm asking you to talk about something else."

He looked at me funny, and I wondered what I'd said wrong. I was always saying something wrong.

"So, you're not mad?"'

"No." I bit my lip. "Why would I be mad?"

"Because you said…" He opened his mouth as if to say something, then closed it again. "Never mind."

I cringed and scratched my elbow. "I'm not like normal people. What I say is pretty much what I mean. I should probably come with a warning sign."

"And what would it say?"'

"Warning: Freak Ahead." I tried to laugh, but it came out more like a choke.

"Nope. Try again."

"Hey! Why didn't you like my sign? It's the truth." I flipped my dark hair over my shoulder and clutched my books and stuff to my chest.

"No."

"What?"

"If you wore a sign, it should say something like, Warning: Cute *and* Smart."

Did he really just say what I think he said? My breathing became erratic, and suddenly, I needed to look at the ground. Study it, even.

"Well, don't you like that one better?" He nudged my shoulder with his elbow. "It's much more you."

I glanced back up. "Why would you say that?"

He shrugged. "Because it's the truth."

I shook my head. Was he out of his mind?

He chuckled and started walking down the road again.

"What's so funny?"

"You."

"Me? Why?"

"I don't know. I can't figure you out, I guess."

Huh? "Why would you want to do that?"

He grinned as he looked over.

I loved the way his hipster hair was combed just right and shone in the sun.

"Why not?"

Why not? I blinked. "What were we talking about?" My face burst into flames. Good grief, had I already lost the conversation *again*?

He tilted his chin and really looked at me. "Ellyn, you have got to be one of the most unique girls I've ever met."

I was in way over my head. "I am?"

"Yep."

"Uh—is that a good thing?"

"Of course!" He grinned that amazing grin again. "Nobody wants the same thing. It's much better if you're unique and stand out. Trust me on this."

Oh, okay. I understood that. "Yeah, I don't really fit in anywhere."

I guess I sounded off or something because he asked, "Why would you use that tone of voice?"

We were almost to my door. Maralyn had already gone in. "What do you mean?"

Zane stared at me for a bit before saying, "You really have no idea how beautiful you are, do you?"

If I was drinking water, I'd have spit it all over him. "What? Are you crazy? Maralyn's the beautiful one. I'm just me."

"Uh …" He laughed. "I hate to point out the obvious, but you're identical twins."

I was lost. Walking up to my front porch, I set my stuff down. "So?"

"Wow." He took off his backpack and set it on the ground near his feet.

Something in the look on his face made my breath catch in my throat.

"How can you look the way you do, yet be still so . . . so ..."

"Weird?"

"Humble."

I stepped back. "Humble?"

"Okay—sweet, then. Why are you not more snobbish, like other pretty girls?"

I laughed and shook my head. This really was getting too much for me. It was time to change the subject. "Well, I made it home. Thanks for walking with me."

"Sure." He got the hint and picked up his backpack again. "Do you mind if I walk home with you again sometime?"

"If you want to. I don't mind."

"Yeah." He took a couple of steps toward the sidewalk. "I think I'd like that."

Was I really going to have a friend this year? "Me too, neighbor." I waved until I noticed that he was heading back the way we came. "Where do you live? I thought it was that way." I pointed past my house.

"Yeah, I do." He looked a bit sheepish before answering, "I—I just have to go back and get my car. It's still at the school."

"What?" I laughed. The dork. "Did you forget that you drove it?"

"No." Zane looked down at his shoes and then back at me. "I just wanted to walk with you."

"Oh." My heart somersaulted. I finally knew what that feeling was like. And man, it was kind of amazing.

"I'll catch you next time."

I smiled as I watched him walk away—the unexpected giddiness nearly overwhelmed me.

"Well, look at you!" Maralyn pushed open the front door. "You've finally got yourself a boyfriend! Wait till I tell Mom."

"Mara, stop. We're just friends."

She raised her eyebrows. "Are you out of your mind? I totally heard him. He left his car at school to walk you home.

That's not *just* friends."

"How do you know?"

She gave me *the* look. "Don't even start. I know when a guy is falling for someone. And that Zane guy is falling all over you."

THREE
♥
CONFUSING MESSES

I walked into the house and set my books on the living room couch before heading into the kitchen. Mom wouldn't be home for another hour or two, and the sink was still a mess from last night. I knew she'd freak out if she came back and our chores *still* weren't done, so after I got a drink, I went to work.

Maralyn didn't even complain when she came over to the dishwasher and began to unload it. Usually, she hated chores, but today, she must've been more curious than she let on. "So, tell me about Zane. How'd you meet him?" she asked after a few minutes.

"He was my tour guide today. The office sent him. Who did you get?"

She shrugged. "This quiet girl. I don't know . . . Janice or something. I don't remember."

"Did she help?"

"Yes." Maralyn placed some cups in the cupboard and then put her hand on her hip. "Okay, out with it. Tell me about him. He's really good-looking. Like, hot."

"Yeah." I really didn't know how to start. Zane was definitely really cute, and not my type. Not that I had a type—I didn't. Just . . . he was a boy. And boys don't usually, ever—

"Um, where'd you go? What'd you talk about? Come on! Tell me about him."

What did she want to know? He was tall, he liked science, he was sweet—but I wasn't even sure what she was asking. This kind of junk drove me nuts. Why do girls—especially my sister—have to know every single detail? Even details I don't know anything about. Sometimes I wonder if she wants me to make stuff up just so she gets an answer she wants to hear. Truth is, I really didn't find out that much about him. I was grateful to hang out, but he had asked all the questions. Not me. "I don't know. He's nice." There. I smiled.

She groaned as she put the plates in the cupboard. "You're the worst. You know that? I can never get *anything* out of you! Anything."

"I said he was nice." Sheesh. I wasn't sure why I tried to talk to her. My elbow began to itch again. I hated itchy elbows. Hated them. And this one was constantly bugging me. I took a deep breath. I slowly wrung out a washcloth and began wiping down the stove.

"Nice isn't always good enough," Maralyn said. "Sometimes you have to actually fill in conversations with words. You know, those things made of letters that turn into stuff that you *say*. Words. Eventually, you put them together, and they become sentences."

My head was beginning to pound. I had no idea why she was so upset with me, but this was ridiculous. All I wanted to do was wipe off the counters and fill the dishwasher like Mom had said. That was it. Why couldn't she see that?

"Really? You're not even going to say anything right now? You're just going to be silent? I know we've never been super close, but could we maybe try for once? You need to talk. If you would just listen to me—"

"Aaaah!" I tossed the rag into the sink. "Stop it. Just stop." I couldn't take another second of this. I hated doing things wrong, and now Maralyn was mad at me and I didn't know why.

"Ellyn …"

I was already walking down the hall. As quickly as I could, I closed our bedroom door and locked it. Then I crawled into the bottom bunk and stared up at the wood above me. *Breathe. Open your mouth and breathe.*

I tried. I tried to calm down. But everything was too crazy and crowded and confusing all at once. I didn't know why Zane followed me home from school, or why he wanted to talk to me, or why he was nice to me. It didn't matter, anyway—in a few days, he was going to see what a weirdo I was, and he wouldn't care about me anymore. Chances are, I'd show my true colors soon enough and do something stupid like lose it and shout and run out of the room and stress out and just … ugh. Why did everybody have to ask so many questions all the time? Why weren't my answers ever good enough?

I never understood it, either. Other people could speak and then those around them would nod and answer back, and everyone would laugh. But with me, it was like my translator got rewired and words would get stuck on their way out of my mouth, and I couldn't really communicate with anyone. At least, not reasonably. They weren't happy with my answers, and it honestly made me want to curl up and not speak sometimes.

I hated it.

At the same time, I wanted so much to have a sister relationship with Maralyn. I loved her more than she knew, and I needed these days when she'd take the time to be nosey and showed she cared about me—it just didn't always go right.

Only Dad had known what to say and how to say it. Even when I flipped out, he'd know and come and talk me out of it and make me giggle again.

I wiped at a couple of rogue tears and then slammed my fist into the mattress beneath me. Why did he have to go? *Why?* It wasn't fair!

I heard Maralyn's knock, but I ignored it. A few seconds later, she asked, "Hey, can I come in?"

That was the other thing which was so hard for us. Even though we were twins, Mom had insisted that we grow up with our own personalities from the beginning, so up until now, we'd both had our own bedrooms. But since Dad died, we couldn't afford more than a two-bedroom home. Mom was already sharing with our eight-year-old sister, Katelyn. That meant Maralyn and I had to learn to share too.

I unlocked the door and walked back to my bed.

Maralyn had insisted on the top bunk, so I got the lower. My only fear was that her bed would fall on me. So far, it hadn't, but some nights I was definitely worried.

She opened the door. "Sorry I got so intense back there."

"I know. I just need a minute."

"Yeah, I figured." She crashed on the floor next to me. "But really, I didn't mean to push you. I just kind of wanted to share some girly stuff with you, I guess."

"I'm not sure I *do* girly stuff. I think you might need one of your other friends."

She moaned and laid her head on the bed. "I don't *have* friends right now, remember? We just moved here."

I hadn't thought about that. While I could stay in this room for days, never speaking to anyone and being perfectly fine, Maralyn couldn't. She needed friends, loved them, and was sort of lost without that constant chattering. "Oh, well, you'll have them really soon."

"Probably. But it doesn't stop the boredom now." She looked up. "So, when you're ready, I'd like to hear about Zane. Or at least, if you like him."

"Sure. He's really nice."

"You already said that."

"But he is!" I chuckled.

"Okay, but what else is he?"

"Um, he's cute."

"Does he play sports? Draw? Love school? Dance? I mean—come on! You were with the guy all day. What's he like? What does he do?"

Deep breath. Deep breath. Breathe. Breathe. Breathe. "Mara, I really don't know what you want me to say. I thought I was telling you."

"Saying he's nice and cute isn't telling me anything. I already knew he was nice and cute the second I met him." She looked at me. "If he asks you out, will you say yes?"

I gulped. "On a date?"

She laughed. "Yes, on a date."

"I—I don't know." Mom let us start dating as soon as we turned sixteen. Of course, Maralyn dated a ton, but now we were both seventeen, and I still hadn't been asked out once.

She got a bit giggly and perked right up. "You have to promise me that you'll say yes if he does. Can you promise that?"

The chances of him ever asking me out were pretty slim—well, to be honest, I had a better chance with him than anyone else. "Okay. Sure. I promise to say yes *if* he asks me out." We both knew he never would. I grinned. This was going to be a piece of cake.

"Good." She clapped her hands and smiled this huge smile.

"Whatever." I rolled my eyes and leaned back on my pillow. "You look like a dork."

She teasingly shook the bed. "Eeeh! Ellyn's got a boyfriend. It's so exciting!"

"What? No. Don't start that." I was beginning to lose my cool again. There really was no place to hide in this tiny house. "I told you already, we're just friends. I mean it."

"Yes, but that's a small technicality. And something that's very easily changed." She got on her knees and pulled her phone out of her pocket. "Watch. What's his number? I'll give him a little call, and by tomorrow morning, you'll totally have him as your B-F."

"Are you kidding me?" I would absolutely die of mortification. "You wouldn't dare!"

She seemed surprised at my vehemence. "What?"

"Mara, put your phone away. I don't have his number. He never gave it to me. And even if he did, I'd *never* give it to you anyway."

"But why? Don't you want a boyfriend?" She looked hurt.

Not if it meant this level of insanity. "No, definitely not. I'm happy the way I am."

Maralyn plopped back down on the floor. "But I don't get it."

"What?"

"You really don't care, do you?"

"About what?"

She threw her hands in the air. "About a guy liking you."

Sure, I cared. I mean, I'd like it if Zane liked me, but I didn't need it. Chances are, he'd turn around and leave eventually anyway. So, really, it just wasn't worth investing in someone who wouldn't be there later. I knew this. I'd spent way too many days of my life worrying if I'd ever have a friend. If the other kids would learn to like me instead of making fun of me. My whole school career was about keeping my head down, attempting to make sense of a world of chaos and drawing as little attention to myself as possible.

I knew they thought I was weird. I was autistic—I wasn't deaf. I heard what they'd said about me. I knew they made fun of me and mocked me, especially when I was younger and used to go off in my own little world and imagine crazy adventure scenes and talk out loud and make exploding noises. I'd forget where I was sometimes and just live in this other place—this magical place where fun things happened. And that's when I got picked on the most.

Thank goodness I didn't stutter as much as before. Speech therapy helped me over that hurdle back when I was really young. Every now and then, I'd get a little excited, sure, and something just wouldn't come out right. But for the most part, I'm pretty much normal. Just a quirky, nerdy, goofy normal.

"Ellyn?"

I blinked. "Yeah?"

"Well, whatever you think, I feel like this is a big day for you—some sort of milestone—and even if you're not going to get all excited about a guy going out of his way to walk you home, I will. This is amazing! And something I've been sort of praying would happen for years now."

"Years?" She was way too dramatic.

"You have no idea." She leaned in and grabbed one of my hands.

I pulled it away.

"This is cool. I'm proud of you. And I totally like that guy now. I do. He's pretty much awesome in my book. I can't wait to see where this goes."

I sighed and closed my eyes. "Mara, it's okay. Even if this goes nowhere, it's okay. We'll all be fine."

"Do you know what I think?"

"What?" I peeked an eye open. I shouldn't have. She was grinning like a fool.

"I think you're secretly totally crushing on him, but you're just too used to hiding to show it."

Was I? I didn't think so. "Not true. I like him, sure. But I'm not crushing."

"*Yet.*" She started to talk faster. "And when you do, you *must*, and I mean M.U.S.T. show him you like him a little bit more than you're showing now. Be outgoing and smile and flirt so he knows how you feel. Okay?"

At this point, I'd say anything to get rid of her. "Okay."

"Good!" She pushed away from the bed and stood up. "And if you need any pointers, let me know!"

FOUR
♥
BUTTERFLIES AND FLURRIES

I really wanted to be left alone, so I waited until I figured the coast was clear before I went to my mom's room and got on her laptop, since Mom and Katelyn wouldn't be home for a while. Mom's purple floral bed was pushed up against the wall under the window, and Katelyn's smaller green one was on the wall next to the closet. They had a long white dresser next to the door. I found the laptop charging on Mom's bed and opened it. I could hear a show in the background. Maralyn was probably watching something on Netflix in the living room.

When I logged onto Facebook, my heart jolted when I noticed I had a friend request from Zane Ferrars. I don't know why I was surprised—I just was.

Once I confirmed it, I instantly did a bit of cyber stalking. Scrolling through his pictures, I was startled to see how many friends he had. It looked like he was always doing something fun— snowboarding, rock climbing, team sports, having barbecues …

Then suddenly, he messaged me. The chime nearly gave me a heart attack. Gah! My pulse raced as I imagined us both thinking about each other at the exact same moment. It was so bizarre, but crazy cool, too.

> *Zane Ferrars: Hey. Thanks for accepting my request so fast. How's it going? Did you survive your first day of school?*

I stared at the message for a few minutes, not sure what to do. No one had ever started a conversation like this with me, and my head was spinning too much to think rationally. After some deep breaths, I decided to respond.

> *Ellyn Dashwood: Yes. I survived today. It was a little disconcerting at first, but I'm pretty sure I'll get the hang of it soon.*

> *Zane Ferrars: You will. It must be hard going to a whole new school and all.*

> *Ellyn Dashwood: Yep.*

Now what should I do? I waited a few seconds and then he responded.

> *Zane Ferrars: I'd like to apologize for putting you on*

the spot earlier. My bad. And I
really feel awful about it.

I scrunched my brow. What was he talking about? I couldn't remember anything.

Ellyn Dashwood: What did you do? When?

Zane Ferrars: Lol. Uh, when I brought up your dad and was asking about him.

Ellyn Dashwood: Oh.

He needed more than that. I rushed to send another response.

Ellyn Dashwood: That's okay. Thanks for dropping the subject and wanting to walk with me.

Zane Ferrars: Thanks for putting up with me. Sorry, I usually don't go completely creepy on people—but you're so interesting. I should probably back away before I scare you for good. Lol.

There went my heart racing again. Eeep. I snuggled into the comforter beneath me and bit my lip.

*Ellyn Dashwood: Why am I so
interesting? I don't understand
why you're not more afraid of
me.* ☺

*Zane Ferrars: *coughs* Afraid of
you? Wow. No! And can't you see
why I'd be so excited to meet you?*

Ha. A totally hot guy like Zane? Yeah, right.

Ellyn Dashwood: Um, no.

*Zane Ferrars: *facepalm* Because
you can keep up. I mean, you're
wrong and all—Edison wasn't
half the genius Tesla was—but
the fact that we can discuss it
seriously is so cool. I've never met
a girl like you.*

"What?" Gah. I pulled up Wikipedia and Thomas Edison.
"There. Read this and weep." I grinned smugly as I pushed
send.

*Ellyn Dashwood: Here. This is
why I'm right. Follow this link.
http://en,wikipedia.org/wiki/
Thomas_Edison*

Zane Ferrars: Lol. Okay. I will. I promise to do so with an open mind, too. But ONLY if you follow this link and watch this awesome video list on Tesla. (I mean, you can read about him on Wikipedia too, but these videos from curiosity. com sum up his coolness the best.) Er—just watch out for language. I can't remember if there is any, and I don't know if you're OK with that or not. Um. Right. Here's the link. Now be prepared to be stunned, amazed/flabbergasted— behold, the mighty Tesla:https:// curiosity.com/learn/nikola-tesla

I chuckled and rolled my eyes. There was no way Tesla was better than Edison.

Ellyn Dashwood: Fine. ☺
Give me a minute.

I clicked on the link and then watched a couple of videos, impressed with the curiosity.com guy's interpretation of Tesla's genius. Tesla really was pretty much amazing. And I was surprised to find that Edison didn't like him at all. I messaged Zane again, this time eating humble pie. Sheesh.

*Ellyn Dashwood: Okay, so I can
see your point. Kind of.*

I didn't want to give him too much leeway.

*Zane Ferrars: Kind of? Kind of?
Ha! You know he's a total genius.
While you were watching that,
I followed the link to Edison. I
have to admit, there were a few
things I didn't know about the
guy, but I still think Tesla won.*

I grinned. I don't know what happened, but Zane
suddenly got a whole lot hotter.

*Ellyn Dashwood: Yeah. Okay.
You win.*

*Zane Ferrars: Wahoo! I knew
it. I knew I would win! I knew
it!!!!!!! Booyeah!*

Booyeah? The dork. I giggled. Like, a completely Maralyn
giggle. It was fun. I decided to try to tease him.

*Ellyn Dashwood: Um, are you
this crazy all the time?*

*Zane Ferrars: Only when pretty
girls admit I'm right. That*

*never happens, so I have to live
in the moment while it lasts.
*fist pump**

My heart flip-flopped and I tried to keep from smiling too much. Maybe Maralyn was right—maybe he did really like me.

Ellyn Dashwood: Whatever.

Zane Ferrars: So, what are you doing right now?

What an odd thing to ask. Wasn't it obvious?

Ellyn Dashwood: Messaging you on Facebook.

Zane Ferrars: Lol. I love literal logic.

Ellyn Dashwood: Well, good, because that's how I roll. ☺

Zane Ferrars: I meant, do you want to hang out in a few? I've got some chores to do for my dad, but when I'm done, I wouldn't mind showing you around Bloomfield or something.

My breath slammed into my throat so hard, I honestly couldn't breathe for a few seconds. Was he asking me out? On a date? As in, wanting to get to know me and be with me and... Was this how easy it was?

My fingers were all over the place as I attempted to type him back. It took about four tries with badly misspelled words before I gave up and typed simply,

Ellyn Dashwood: OK

Zane Ferrars: Cool. I'll see you in about an hour. Will that work?

I honestly couldn't breathe.

Ellyn Dashwood: Sure.

I had no idea if it would work or not, but I certainly wasn't turning down my first date ever.

Zane Ferrars: Great. Well, I've got to run so I can get there in time. So, catch ya on the flip side. Bye.

Ellyn Dashwood: Bye.

I signed out of Facebook and turned the laptop off. Holy cow. Holy cow. Holy cow. I got off the bed and walked to my room, then back to my mom's, then back to mine again. What was I doing? I needed to get ready.

I went into the bathroom and stared in the mirror for a minute. I really had no idea what to do. Closing my eyes, I finally gave up and called, "Mara, I need your help."

"What?" She asked as she leaned against the doorframe.

When I looked at her, her eyebrows rose. "What's going on? Is everything okay?"

No. I didn't know the first thing about dating. What did I do? What did he do? Was I dressed okay? "Help."

"What is it?"

You've got to speak. Calm down. Say the words so she understands. Thankfully, my mouth opened. "Zane wants to take me to see Bloomfield. Now. In an hour. Like, right now."

Her jaw dropped. "No way."

"Yeah." I nodded.

Suddenly, she screeched. "Eeek! Makeover. Ellyn's got a date!"

In that moment, I believe I was more afraid of my sister than I was of Zane. "Okay, no sudden loud noises. And let's keep this looking like me. I know we're twins, but you're way prettier, so I've still got to look like me and not you."

She tilted her head and gave me a funny look. "I'm going to take that as a compliment."

I blinked. My darn elbow itched again. "Okay. Probably safer that way."

She took a deep breath. "Never mind. We've only got an hour. Where's my makeup?"

I cringed. The last time I'd worn makeup was when I was coerced into the third-grade play.

"Hush. It'll be good for you."

By the time Maralyn had finished attacking my face, I had to say, I didn't look too bad. Turning my head from side to side in the mirror, I checked out her handiwork. She'd made my bangs look cute and textured, and even found an adorable headband. The makeup looked pretty, actually. I smiled at the girl grinning back at me. Bright eyes, long, dark lashes, and just a hint of light pink lip gloss. "Thanks for not overdoing it."

Maralyn laughed. "I'm saving the smoky-eye look for the next date."

I had no idea what that meant, but it sounded painful. "Please don't."

She nudged me with her shoulder. "Hey, I'm just teasing."

Taking a deep breath, I reminded myself for the thousandth time that month that sarcasm was actually a thing people chose to use. It made absolutely no sense to me why anyone would choose to say something besides what they meant—not to mention, completely confusing—but whatever. The world was a weird place.

"Okay. Let's get you changed into clothes that'll match that headband."

I followed her into our bedroom. "Don't I look good enough?" Glancing down at my jeans and T-shirt, I didn't see anything wrong.

She shrugged. "You look fine if you're going to school, but this isn't school. This is Zane Ferrars."

"I really don't want to be uncomfortable. You know how I get with my clothes."

When I was little, it was awful. I hated certain collars and tags and pants and even socks. Basically, anything that didn't feel right on my skin used to bug me so badly, I'd cry until my mom let me change.

"How about this fabric?" Maralyn pulled out a pretty

flowy top of hers for me to borrow.

I touched the white sleeve. The material was soft and smooth. "It might work."

She tossed it at me. "Well, try it on and see." Then she threw me a dark blue ball. "And put these jeans on, too."

I groaned, but quickly changed. I hated the jeans the second I put them on. They were too tight and too flashy, way too trendy-looking for my taste. "The blouse is nice, but I can't do the bottoms. These are just way too close-fitting." I plucked at the fabric that hugged my thighs.

"They're skinny jeans. They're supposed to be snug. Just wear them. They look killer on you."

"No."

"Yes." She put her hands on her hips. "Come on, Ellyn. You can't hide from discomfort your whole life. Sometimes you've gotta go out on a limb and wear something constricting just so you know what the rest of the planet feels like."

"But it'll be too distracting, and I won't be able to concentrate on anything else. And then the date will be a huge failure. I'd rather wear my yoga pants."

Maralyn threw her head back and groaned. "Fine. Put on your jeans." She pointed to where they lay on the floor. "At least they're better than your yoga pants." She walked over to her jewelry box and pulled out a long necklace with a heart at the bottom. "Could you wear this?"

It was really cute. "Maybe."

"Well, let's see." She slipped it over my neck and stepped back. "So, what do you think?"

We shut the bedroom door so I could see in the full-length mirror behind it.

A beautiful dark-haired stranger looked back at me.

"Wow. I don't even look like me."

"Sure you do." She smiled. "It looks just like you—only thing is, you've been hiding."

Mom pushed the door open, and we both jumped. "Hey, girls. What's going on in here?"

"You scared us!" Maralyn gasped.

Mom chuckled. "Good. You need to be scared sometimes." Then she looked over at me. Her tired eyes went from the top to the bottom of my outfit. "Ooh ... I like it. Makeup, even. What's the occasion?"

Maralyn clapped her hands. "Ellyn's got her first date! She's leaving in like, fifteen minutes or so."

"What?" Mom gave us both a stunned gape. "Congratulations, Ellyn." Then she said the last thing I'd expect from her. "But no, you're not leaving this house. No way. Not yet. Dream on."

"Why?" My face fell.

"Mom!" Maralyn protested.

"Because no one is going anywhere until their jobs are done. And that kitchen is still a disaster." She dropped her purse from her shoulder and ran her fingers through her hair, releasing a few bobby pins. "Now that I'm working full-time, you know you guys need to pitch in. I can't do it all anymore, and I'm not going to." She pointed to the kitchen. "So move it. Both of you. Katelyn's already begun sweeping in there."

Since Mom worked at an elementary school in Farmington, she'd enrolled Katelyn there, so they drive down together.

"I'm sorry. After it's clean, can I go?" I asked. Would she really ruin this chance I had with a guy before it even began?

"We'll see. But as of right now, you're stuck here. Besides, nobody's planning anything without me meeting the guy first."

FIVE

♥

CHAMPION'S CAUSE

Maralyn stepped in front of me and tried to calm Mom down. "Okay. I know you're tired. I think today has been rough for everyone. But Mom, you've got to let Ellyn go on this date. Zane is a really great guy. We promise to let you meet him first—we definitely weren't planning on Ellyn going anywhere until you did."

Actually, I'd completely forgotten about my mom, but I wasn't going to say anything.

Maralyn continued, "And this may be Ellyn's only chance to truly fit in here at this high school. Zane is cute and he likes her, and I swear I'll do all Ellyn's jobs while she's gone."

"What?" I asked.

Mom blinked. "Yeah—what did you say?"

Maralyn rolled her eyes. "Come on. Me offering to do her jobs isn't that rare."

I laughed. "Yes, it is. And thank you."

Mom put a hand on her hip and raised an eyebrow. "Okay, what gives? Why are you being so dramatic?"

"Because this is epic!" Maralyn exclaimed.

Mom winked at me. "I know it is. But it's just a date. Jobs are important too, you know. Especially when people are coming over and will see this dirty house." She cleared her throat. Mom always cleared her throat when she was mad.

Maralyn groaned. "You'll never understand." She walked past us. "Fine, I'll start cleaning now. And I wasn't kidding about doing Ellyn's stuff too. You know how she is—she's going to need time to reflect and get ready for this date."

As Maralyn walked out of the room, still grumbling, Mom turned to me. "Okay, so tell me the truth. Do you want to do this? Or is your sister setting you up and trying to coerce you into getting out of your shell?"

I guess it would seem that way. "Yes, I want to. I think. I'm kind of nervous. And Zane asked me out all on his own—Maralyn didn't even know until I told her." My elbow began to itch again. "But I don't know if it's really a date. He only asked to take me around Bloomfield so I could get to know the area better. We're just friends."

She walked over to the pink fluffy chair by the window and sat down. "So, let me get this straight. You went to school today for the first time, and already, a boy has asked you to drive around town."

"Yeah."

"And you met him at school?"

"He was the guide who was assigned by the office to help me get to my classes."

She nodded and smiled. "Okay. Then you need to understand something. If a boy asks to spend time with you, even just as friends—which is how all relationships should start—then he likes you and wants to get to know you more, even if he doesn't realize it yet. It's a date. At least, you can use it for practice." She tucked a strand of her hair behind her ear. "Do you like him?"

I shrugged. "I don't know. I guess. He's nice. More surprising than anything, really."

"Why's that?"

My eyes got big. How could she not know this? "Well, because I'm not really the type the male gender wants to hang out with."

"Good grief. You're as dramatic as Mara sometimes. You know perfectly well there are many males who like you."

I laughed. "Whatever. Male cats and dogs don't count."

Mom tilted her head and looked at me seriously for a minute. "Do you really believe boys aren't attracted to your type? Did that actually come out of your mouth?"

Was this a trick question? "Yes."

"It concerns me that you believe this about yourself." She patted her knee. "Come here."

"Mom, I'm taller than you are. I'm not sitting on your knee."

"Excuse me, young lady. I am and will always be your mom. Now sit down and let's talk for a second."

I sighed and awkwardly perched on her legs.

"There. See?"

She wrapped an arm around me, and I tried really hard not to flinch or squirm. What was it about someone touching me that sort of freaked me out?

"I love you. Do you know that?"

Okay. So this was going to be one of *those* moments. "Yeah. I love you too, Mom."

"You are amazing and stunningly beautiful, and any boy at your school would be a fool not to notice the great things about you."

"It would seem there are a lot of fools, then."

She sighed. "Ellie, stop. You're driving me crazy."

I said what Dad always said to her. "I fear it was a short drive."

Mom laughed. "Enough." She squeezed me tight and then said, "I miss him too, you know."

I relaxed a bit and rested my head on hers. "I know."

"He would always know what to say, wouldn't he? You two were so close."

I nodded and felt strands of her hair brush my cheek.

"What would he have said to you just now if he heard what you really think about yourself?"

I shrugged and then sat up. "I don't know. Probably something about how pretty I am and how boys are stupid and don't realize what's right in front of them until it's gone. He'd crack some sort of joke to make me smile. And then he'd ask me if there was any guy I liked."

"And what would you say if he asked you that right now?"

I took a deep breath. "I'd say, not really. But there was this new guy who seemed to like me, and he walked me home from school and talked to me about scientists, and he said I'm a genius because I have autism."

"Really?" Mom seemed shocked, but she quickly covered it up. "What do you think Dad would've said to that?"

I grinned. "That Zane sounds very intelligent and like the perfect boy to try out all his dating scare tactics on, and that I should bring him over. He'll be sure to clean his gun."

She chuckled and then asked quietly, "Would Dad like him?"

"Yeah, I think so."

"I think so too. In fact, I'm kind of curious about him now. When is he coming over?"

I glanced at my alarm clock. "In about ten minutes."

"And are you ready to drive around the area with him? Do you feel safe?"

Safe? "What do you mean?"

"I'm just making sure he isn't sending off any creepy vibes and that you're completely comfortable with the idea of hanging out with him. Since this will be your first real date."

I was pretty sure I'd never be comfortable on a date. "No creepy vibes. And I don't think it's possible to be relaxed when you're getting to know a cute person."

"You've got a point." Mom squeezed me again, and then after a few minutes said something quietly to sober the mood a bit. But I guess, in a way, it needed to be said. "You—you don't think this is a joke, do you? Some sort of bullying?"

It's exactly what I feared most. I closed my eyes and swallowed the lump in my throat. "I hope not." I'd gotten pretty used to the odd looks and the mimicking echoes in class, as well as the giggles and whispers as people walked past and glanced back at me in the halls. I already knew what it was like to be excluded from the awesomeness of Maralyn's friends. She always tried her best to include me, but I knew I'd never feel comfortable around a group of people who'd mock me as soon as my sister turned away.

That was probably the worst thing about having autism. Just. Not. Fitting. In. The cruel reality that tells you every day that you're not worth being around. That just because you talk differently and think differently, you're stupid, ugly, freakishly weird, and basically a nuisance.

Lunches were always alone. Homework, study groups, sitting in class… I was always by myself. No one to share my frustrations with, my excitements of the day, or even laugh with me when something silly happened. Only my dad tried to be there.

He was my best friend.

And now he was gone.

I sat in my room a lot thinking late at night, wondering why the universe would choose to take him from me. Was I always supposed to be alone?

"Hey, you okay?" Mom jiggled me a little. "I'm sorry. I should've never mentioned the bullying thing. I'm sure this guy is legit. Don't worry about it."

I sniffed and wiped my eyes with the back of my hand. "Yeah. It'll be fine." Very slowly, I pulled out of her arms. "Can I get a few minutes by myself? I just need to think for a minute. Is that okay?"

"Of course." She stood up. "I'll call you when he gets here." When she got to the door, she turned back. "Ellie?"

I looked up. "What?"

Mom searched my eyes for a few seconds and then shook her head. "Never mind. Take some time for you, and we'll talk later. I love you."

"I love you too."

When the door shut, I gave a huge sigh of relief and plopped down on my bed. I stared up at the wooden beams below Maralyn's bunk and just waited. If I was really still for a while, my heart would eventually release all the heaviness, and then my breathing would get better and I could just relax. The pain was still too real and fresh to disappear completely, but at least I'd balance what I could.

After a few minutes of processing, I began to wonder about Zane again. I hoped with every bit of me that it was really happening, and that he wasn't some jerk or something.

However, it was pointless to imagine the worst when there was no evidence of it yet. And it was hopeless to believe there was anything more than just friendship here either. The reality—as I knew it—was that a nice guy wanted me to feel welcome in Bloomfield. That was it. And if anything worse came of it—well, it wouldn't be the first time. And if anything better came of it—then . . . then . . . yeah. I might just die. But there was no reason to get all worked up until I knew for sure. Period.

By the time my mom knocked on the door to let me know he was there, my heart was beating normally again and I was ready to face whatever fate came my way. After straightening my clothes and hair, I walked into the living room.

"Hey, Ellyn." Zane's smile brightened the whole room. "You look great!"

SIX

ZANE & ELLYN
SITTIN' IN A TREE

After the introductions were made and the odd chitchat over with, Mom finally let us head out of the house.

"Your family is nice," Zane said as he opened the car door for me.

"Thanks." I climbed in and waited until he entered on the other side before speaking again. "You're sweet for saying that."

"What?" He started the car. "It was fun getting to know them."

I fiddled with my seatbelt and then looked around, deciding to change the subject. "So, is this your car?" I didn't notice the outside when I got in, but the interior looked ridiculously new. Too nice for your typical high-school kid. It had the feel of something a rich businessman would drive.

"Yep. She's mine, all right. My dad said he'd match whatever I saved toward a car. For two years, I put every penny away so when it came time to buy it, I think I surprised him." He gunned the gas a little as he headed down the road. Nothing scary, or even above the speed limit. However, it made an impressive sound.

"This car looks much more expensive than anything we've ever owned. What is it?"

He looked a bit sheepish and then replied, "Tesla Model S."

"Wait—what? Tesla invented cars, too?"

"No. This is just Tesla Motors. They named their company after him because of his inventions, and they thought he was a pretty cool dude."

"Oh." I wasn't sure what to say.

"It's an electric car."

Now things were beginning to make sense. "Not bad."

He grinned. "Yeah, Tesla Motors is making history. This is the only completely electric car on the market. They even have recharging stations in almost all the cities."

"Wow. I didn't know they made those."

"My dad was shocked. He thought I'd be all over a sports car or something."

"But you chose a much more practical car." Now I was even more curious than before. "So, you said you work for your dad. What does he do?"

"He sells cars, actually. We were able to get a discount for this one."

"Oh. Do you like working for him?"

He shrugged. "I don't know. My dad's been pushing me to get a business degree so I can take over the dealership one day."

"Wow. You guys have your own dealership and everything? You must really like cars, then."

"Sure, as much as the next guy. I mean, don't get me wrong. I love driving this car around, but I wouldn't say it's my passion to sell them to people or anything."

"Wait. You don't want to take over your dad's business?" Was he crazy? It seemed to be successful enough, if he could afford to pay for half of his son's brand-new car.

"No, I'd rather get a degree in biophysics or biochemistry, something that continues to enhance and change the world. Maybe find the cure for some disease or something."

Now he was speaking my language. I smiled.

"What? You don't like that?"

How was I always sending off the wrong signals? "No, I love it. I . . . I was just thinking how similar we are."

"Oh, sorry. My dad thinks I'm a loser for setting my sights so high. He sort of laughs at me. He thinks those kinds of goals are a waste of time, especially since he already owns a thriving business and I wouldn't need to spend years in college learning a skill I'd never use."

"Huh."

"Never mind. Let's not think about my dad and work and junk. Instead, let's focus on the awesomeness of your new city."

While he continued to chat, I did just the opposite and thought about Zane's life. I couldn't help myself—it was a puzzle that made no sense to me. I couldn't imagine a man not wanting his son to learn. As in, he actually wanted his son to stay home and never challenge himself. It seemed so odd. My dad had always encouraged me to grow and develop every day. He wanted me to have a normal life of challenges and of chasing my dreams. Zane's relationship with his father seemed pretty sad.

"Hey, you're really quiet. Did I bore you, talking about my family? You haven't said much since."

I blinked. It took me a minute to catch what he was saying. "Sorry, no. I'm not bored. Not at all." I glanced out the window at the different shops. Bloomfield had more stores and restaurants than I'd imagined it would. "I was just..." I trailed off as I compared Zane's life to mine again.

"You were just...?"

"Huh?"

"You stopped talking. I was wondering what you were going to say."

"I did?" I laughed nervously. My elbow began to itch again. "Sorry. I really like the buildings and stuff. Thank you for showing me." All at once, I wanted to go home so I could sort out Zane's mess. What if he were to talk to his dad and really explain things to him? Or better yet, show his dad the amazing things biophysics could do for the world—or biochemistry, for that matter. Knowing his love and fascination for science, there was no limit to what Zane was capable of doing. Why couldn't his dad see that?

After a few minutes, he said, "Ellyn?"

I bit my lip. Dang it, I'd forgotten he was there again. "Yes?"

"Would you like to go home?"

Yes! "Uh..." Wait. What was the right thing to say here? I could never remember the rules. Something was bound to hurt Zane's feelings, but I couldn't understand what. He asked if I wanted to go home. That meant it was okay, didn't it? "Yeah, I'd like to."

He nodded his head and then asked, "Are you mad at me?"

"No, not at all."

"Oh, okay. You seem a bit quiet, is all."

"I'm really not here right now. I'm thinking way too

much."

"I can see that." He gave a lopsided grin. "Can I ask what you're thinking about?"

"You."

He seemed surprised. "Me?" A quick chuckle burst from him. "I don't believe you."

Why wouldn't he? "It's true."

"Really?"

"Yep."

"And just *what* are you thinking about me? Ways to kill me or something?"

I nearly choked. What in the world was he talking about? I'd never kill him. Ever. Unless he hurt a cat or my family or turned into a creepy weirdo—was he a weirdo?—and . . . and I really wanted to go home now.

"I'm kidding," he said. "I was just trying to tease you."

"Oh." I must've looked really nervous because he pulled into the empty lot of a church and parked.

"I'm sorry." Zane turned toward me. "Let's start again. What were you thinking about?"

Why did we stop? "I was worried about your dad not wanting you to go to college."

"Really?"

"I was trying to think of a way to get him to change his mind."

"Why?" His eyes stared into mine.

I quickly looked away. "So you could be happy." My heart started to pound. It's like it finally dawned on me. I was out with a really cute guy, and he'd stopped the car and was looking at me, and ... All at once, I was totally nervous. I'd seen this move a hundred times in the movies. This is when the guy kisses you, isn't it?

Zane scrunched his eyebrows and shook his head. "Where did you come from, Ellyn Dashwood?"

"Um...?" Did he really want to know?

"You're amazing."

Oh, my gosh! This was it. This was when he'd kiss me. I wasn't even sure what I'd done to make him want to, or why, but I licked my lips and held my hands so they wouldn't shake.

Zane's eyes were still looking at me. He hadn't moved. "I wish there was a way to get my dad to see me like that."

"Are you going to kiss me?" Gah! Why did I say that? My hand flew to my mouth as I went bright red.

He laughed. "Um, I wasn't planning on it. But I have thought about it today."

"Sorry!" I was so embarrassed, I almost didn't catch the last part. "Wait. What? You have?"

"Yeah, a few times."

"You've thought about kissing me?"

He sighed. "Yes, but I shouldn't. Do you have a boyfriend?"

"A what?"

"You know, from your last school?"

Was he out of his mind? "No. I'm not really the boyfriend type, remember?"

He looked at me for a minute before he spoke. "I think you'd make the perfect girlfriend."

My heart somersaulted in my chest. I couldn't even say a word even if I wanted to. Was he asking me to be his girlfriend? As in, right now? Is this what that was like? Holy cow.

Suddenly, his phone began to ring.

"Ellyn, there's something I need to say."

"Okay." His phone still rang.

"You know how when you're young, you do stupid things?" Huh? That was the last thing I expected him to say. "Yeah."

"Well, I'd always wanted a girlfriend, from the time I was in sixth grade. It was kind of a goal of mine to get one."

He actually said "girlfriend" again. I smiled. The phone wouldn't stop ringing.

"So when I met you…" He glanced down at the phone. "Oh, shoot. This is my mom. Hang on."

I attempted to calm my pounding heart and nerves while he talked to her.

"Dang! Was that today? So sorry. I totally forgot. I'll head home now." He put the car in reverse and backed out of the parking lot. "Is everyone else over there right now?"

He listened for a moment and then glanced at me. "I'm with a friend. I'll drop her off and head over there."

I guess this date's over. It didn't matter. The guy I was beginning to crush on nearly asked me to be his girlfriend. That had to count for something, didn't it? That *never* happened to me. What were the odds that the guy I liked liked me too? It was crazy.

"Sorry about that." Zane set the phone down and then pulled into traffic. "My mom needs me home as soon as possible." He headed straight toward my street. "I hope you had fun today."

"I did. Thank you." Grinning, I watched the buildings pass by through the window. "This has to go down on the record as the best first day of school day ever."

"Ever, huh?" He raised a brow and then looked back to the road. "Glad you liked it. It's been fun getting to know you. Bloomfield High definitely won't be the same now that you've moved in."

"You're pretty amazing yourself."

"Me?" He shook his head. "Nah, once you get to know me, you'll realize I'm your typical geek, through and through."

"And that's what I find so cool!"

He pulled up in front of my house. "Then I'd say we've definitely got something here."

I grinned and opened the door. "You think?" I knew he had to go, and I didn't want to make him even later than he was. "Thanks so much for showing me around."

"No worries. I'll see you tomorrow."

"Okay."

Without another word, I headed up to the house. By the time I'd turned back to close the door behind me, he was already gone. I could hear my mom call out, "Hey, Ellyn. That was short. How was it?" But I didn't answer her. Not yet. I needed to be alone for a few minutes to gather my thoughts. I locked my bedroom door, crawled into bed, and stared up at Maralyn's bunk. Then slowly, I began to breathe again. Long, deep breaths. Was this really happening to me? Was I about to get my very own boyfriend? My emotions were jumbled just thinking about it. I wanted to squeal and giggle and act like a weird version of Maralyn. Not that I would—it really wasn't my style—but I definitely began to see why she did.

Maybe this world wasn't so bad after all.

And maybe my dad was right—maybe there were some great guys out there.

I imagined Dad and Zane meeting and chuckled. Of course Dad would love him. How could he not?

Zane was absolutely perfect.

SEVEN

♥

DEVIL'S ADVOCATE

The next morning, my little sister, Katelyn, bounded into our room, and like a typical eight-year-old, she jumped on my bed. "When's Zane coming back over?" she asked as she belly flopped right on me.

"Oomph!" I moaned and rolled over. Katelyn managed to remain on top of me. "Good grief. When did you get so big?"

"Zane! Zane!" She started bouncing. "I want Zane!"

I could hear Maralyn move above us. "Katelyn, go away. It's too early in the morning for this."

"Why do you want Zane?" I asked. I didn't realize she cared that much.

"Because Mara says you're going to marry him someday."

"What?" Maralyn and I both said at the same time.

"I did not." Mara tossed down a yellow pillow. It ricocheted off the side of the bed and landed on the dresser.

"Uh-huh." Katelyn was going to make me sick with all

this bouncing. "You said that he loved Ellie and they were going to be together forever."

How could this family move so fast? I was barely processing that I liked the guy and they were already marrying me off. I groaned. "Not true. We're just friends."

"That's not what Mara says. She says you're—"

Maralyn popped her head over the side. "All right, monster. Get off Ellie and go get ready for school."

"But I want to see Zane again."

"Leave her alone." Maralyn chucked another yellow pillow. This time, it bounced off Katelyn. "Ellie, you know you can tell her to get up."

I knew I could, but I wasn't sure how to do it without being mean. Besides, how many big sisters get to have this kind of attention from their little sisters? I grabbed Katelyn and began to tickle her. "Why are you so nosey, huh?" I asked around her squeals and giggles.

"Ugh." Maralyn flung herself up on her bed. "You guys are going to make sure we don't get any more sleep today."

Katelyn and I both ignored her until I finally let up, and we each sighed in relief. Then she snuggled her way up to me as I lay back on my pillow. "I think Zane is nice. I like him."

I ruffled her hair. "Me too." Her bright blues eyes looked at me. Nobody should ever be this happy so early in the morning. There should be a law against it. "But why do you like him so much? You hardly got to see him."

"I know." She flipped around and looked up at Maralyn's bunk with me. "That's why he needs to come over. If you're going to marry him, we need to know him better."

"Ah, I see. Well, what if I told you I wasn't going to marry him?"

"Then he needs to come over more so he falls in love with you and then asks you to marry him."

If only life were that simple. Heck, forget marriage—I'd be happy enough if the guy asked me to prom.

Katelyn brought the comforter up to her chin. "I'm not leaving until you say he's coming over again."

"How about if I promise that the next time I see him, I'll invite him to our house?"

"Nope." She shook her head. "That's not good enough. I need to know he'll be back for sure."

I grinned. "Katelyn, life isn't about already knowing what's going to happen to us before we wake up. It's about going slow and steady and experiencing everything out there at the time it's supposed to be there. Don't rush anything. Just sit back and enjoy it."

I could tell she was way too much like Maralyn to agree with any of that. "I don't understand everything you said right now, but it doesn't matter. I like things to come fast. I don't like waiting."

Maralyn chuckled. "Smart girl."

I tossed the pillow back up at her. "Hey, don't encourage another Dashwood. I don't think Bloomfield could handle one more."

"So, have any new feelings developed for Zane yet?" Maralyn asked.

I shrugged, even though she couldn't see me. "I still like him, if that's what you mean."

She grumbled something and then climbed off the bed. "You're hopeless."

"What do you expect me to say? That I'm picking out my wedding dress?"

"Wedding dress?" Katelyn smiled.

"Er, it was just a joke," I tried to protest.

"I want you to admit that you have feelings for him, out loud, so we can move on to the next step."

"Next step?" What was she talking about? And honestly, there was no way I was going to admit anything to anyone out loud. With my luck, I'd lose him just as soon as I opened my mouth to speak.

"You know—getting Zane to ask you out so you can show off to the school that you have a boyfriend."

I sighed, gently pulled away from Katelyn, and got out of bed. Between the two of them, this was going to be one long day. Thankfully, I'd be spending most of it at school.

The day only seemed to get longer once I was at school. In fact, by the time I'd said good-bye to Zane and walked into my second-hour class, I'd pretty much decided this day was never going to end.

"Hi. So, you're new, right?" A pretty girl with light brown hair sitting at the desk on my left was looking right at me.

I wouldn't have believed she was talking to me, but I was sure I was the only new kid in this class. I set my laptop on the desk and put my bag on the floor. "Yes."

"Ellyn?"

And she knew my name. It was always awkward when someone knew me but I didn't know them. "Yes."

She smiled brightly as I sat down. I wasn't sure what to say next.

"How do you like the school?"

"Um, it's okay." I glanced around and noticed the place was still pretty empty. The warning bell hadn't rung yet.

"Good." She looked a little nervous. I wasn't sure if it was me making her nervous or something else. And then she blurted out the craziest thing. "So, I see that you and Zane seem to know each other already. Are you old family friends or something?"

"Uh, no. I just met him yesterday."

"Yesterday?" She laughed loudly.

I wasn't sure what was so funny, but the laugh was too forced, like she had hidden anger issues or something. People were beginning to stare, so I opened my laptop and tried to ignore her.

"Do you know what?"

I looked up. "What?"

"I think I like you."

She didn't even know me. "Thanks."

"I think we're going to get along and be friends in no time."

I seriously had my doubts. "Oh." This must have been the oddest conversation I'd ever had. Okay, it probably wasn't—I had some real doozies sometimes—but this had to rank in the top ten.

"So, how did you meet Zane?"

Why did I feel like I was being grilled all of a sudden? "He was my aide yesterday to show me around school."

The girl flipped her hair over her shoulder as the warning bell went off. "That makes sense." Then she leaned over and whispered, "I'm Loni, by the way."

"Hi." Where were my manners? That's probably why she was acting like this. "Sorry. I should've asked you earlier."

"Asked me what?"

"Your name."

She brushed it aside. "No, that's fine. So, I was wondering—

did you and Zane spend all day together yesterday? Someone mentioned that he walked you home from school."

"We didn't spend all day together, but yeah, he walked me home."

"Was something wrong with his car, then?"

"No. Why?"

She shrugged and popped a piece of gum in her mouth. "Just curious. I'm surprised that he left his car at school."

I grinned, and my heart sort of grew a bit. "Yeah, he's really sweet."

Loni's eyes met mine, and she smacked her gum. "He is. *Really* sweet."

I wasn't sure what to say, so I just nodded.

"But if you didn't spend all day with him, why was he late to the family party at his house last night? Wasn't he with you?"

Did this girl know everything? "Were you there?" And then it dawned on me. "Oh, are you Zane's sister?"

"His sister!" She looked shocked. "No. Not even. He doesn't have one."

Just then, the second bell rang. Students clambered to their seats as the teacher stood up. "Hey, class. Today we're going to continue to discuss chapter thirteen. If you could all pull it up on your computers—and make sure it's the chapter thirteen for history, not language arts."

Everybody around me chuckled, and then a guy near the front protested a little bit. "Hey, I only did it twice!" Poor guy. I knew what that was like.

Suddenly, Loni dropped her bag, and scrambled around the side of her desk to pick it up. She knelt right next to me.

I noticed the teacher was writing something on the board.

As Loni collected the bag, she whispered, "Zane said he was with you last night, and that's why he was late to his family thing. Were you guys on a date or something?"

"I wouldn't call it a date." Seriously, this girl was beginning to bug me. "Why do you ask?"

"Because he's a really nice guy with a big heart, and girls tend to take it the wrong way."

My chest began to grow cold. "What you mean?"

"I mean, he's pretty much amazing, and girls fall for him all the time. What's not to fall for, right?"

I swallowed. Was she warning me off? "I don't know."

"And fact is, he's not supposed to be dating anyone. Ever."

"He's not? Why?"

"Because his dad is a controlling loser." Her eyes flashed with rage before glossing over again. "Apparently, he's on a date fast until he agrees to see things his dad's way. So no girls at all until Zane drops this idea of becoming a scientist."

Could anyone really be that cruel? "Are you kidding me? He can't date until he becomes a—"

"Until he agrees to take over his dad's chain of car dealerships, yes. His dad is a millionaire, and he wants the same for Zane."

"But Zane hates selling cars! He'd be miserable."

Her sharp gaze connected with mine again. Those eyes searched me for a second. "That's why it's a huge secret. You have to promise me not to tell anyone at all, or he'd be grounded from prom. And that can't happen!"

"What's the secret?"

She ducked her head and quickly collected her things.

"Loni Steele, do you need some help there?" the teacher asked from the front of the room.

I glanced up and met the teacher's gaze straight on as she continued, "Or perhaps you'd like to keep speaking with Ellyn Dashwood, since apparently, that has become much more important than class. Would either of you like to share what you're talking about?"

Loni stood up. "Sorry. I was just asking if I'd hurt her when my stuff fell."

The teacher's dark eyebrow rose, but she didn't say anything.

Clutching her laptop, Loni quickly sat down. As soon as the teacher began to write on the board again, she leaned over and whispered frantically, "Don't tell anyone, ever, that I'm Zane's girlfriend."

EIGHT
♥
BUCKET OF ICE

I was pretty much numb when I walked out of class. I tried to slap on a smile, but I wasn't sure I had succeeded.

"Ellie! Ellie!" I heard Maralyn down the hallway before I could see her.

"There you are," she exclaimed as she weaved her way through everyone heading to their next class. "I've been looking everywhere for you."

"Why? What's going on?"

She pulled me around the corner into a small alcove between the office and classrooms.

This so wasn't like her. Maralyn never came to find me during school. Suddenly, my stomach clenched. Oh, my gosh. Did something happen to Mom or Katelyn? "What's wrong? Is everyone okay?" Why was she grinning at me like this?

"I know we're in the middle of school and all, but there's a guy in my business math class I had to tell someone about! Since I don't have any best friends right now and you're my most favorite sister, I had to come find you. Gah! I think I'm in love."

"Wait. What?" I blinked, not sure I heard her right. Was something wrong or not?

"A guy! Eeeh!" She clasped her hands together. "He's so perfect, too."

Oh. Relief poured over me. Figures it would be about her latest crush. "Okay. That's nice." *Why does she do this to me?* "Is he taking you out?"

She laughed. "He doesn't even know I exist yet." Then she waggled her brows. "Give me a few more hours, and he'll be mine soon enough."

Of course he would be. "So, what's so exciting?"

"I don't know. My heart was racing, and I was so happy to finally find someone in this school who could do that to me. Sure, there are some hot guys here, but none of them have that 'wow' factor. His name is Harrison Crawford, and he was out of school yesterday, which is why I didn't see him until today. Now all I have to do is get him to notice me, and then everything will be awesome."

"His name is Harrison?"

"Yep."

"As in, Harrison Ford, the *Star Wars* guy?"

She looked at me funny. "Yeah, I guess."

I still couldn't believe she'd scared me like that just to tell me about a cute guy. "Huh. It's a weird name."

"No, it's not! It's an incredible name. It's like a movie-star-romantic name."

I think my jawed dropped. If it didn't, it should have. How could she and I be so different? Seriously. I didn't even have to say a word. She caught on that I wasn't excited.

I could see her happy face slipping a little. "Okay. Well, the bell's gonna ring any minute now. I just wanted to come tell you my news."

A part of me began to feel a little bit guilty. I mean, how many sisters go out of their way to find each other and share stuff like this? I attempted a grin, even though my own issues and the scare were sending conflicting signals. "Hey, thanks for sharing. Sorry, I don't mean to be mean or anything, but I've got a lot going on right now. Let me know when he asks you out. It'll be fun to meet him."

She beamed back to life. "Oh, you'll love him. I'm sure of it!"

"Probably," I lied.

"And when I catch him, we can go on double dates with you and Zane. This will be perfect!"

Thankfully, she ran off before the reality of what she'd said completely registered. Yeah, I finally seem to go somewhere with someone, and bam! I was right where I knew I'd be. Alone. All at once, I was consumed by this stupid urge to cry for no reason. Good grief. I blinked my eyes and leaned back against the wall, hidden by a tall fake plant thingy. The warning bell rang, and I closed my eyes. For the first time ever, even when I was being bullied, I wished I had the guts to ditch school.

I didn't know what my problem was. It wasn't like I hadn't prepared for this sort of thing. It wasn't like I didn't know all along. Getting my hopes up only ever brought pain.

So why let it get to me now? I took a deep breath as the final bell rang. It was only a day we were talking about, anyway. It's not like I'd had months to fall for him. One day. That's it. I was an idiot, and this was over. Kaput. Final.

Time to face this world like a big girl. Squaring my shoulders, I sniffed and walked out of the alcove with my head held high.

And ran right into Zane's chest. Gah!

"Hey, are you all right?" He pulled away. "I was just looking for you. I didn't see you go into chemistry, so I wanted to make sure you weren't lost."

I quickly brushed at my hair and put on a smile. "Yeah, I'm good. How are you?"

"Uh, so *are* you lost? Do you need help?"

I pointed toward the end of the hall. "I don't think so. It's down there, right?"

He looked over. "Yep. That's the right way."

Then we both just stood there. Saying nothing. Because what do you say to the one person you wish you could have, but can't? Nothing. It's just smarter that way. "Where's your class?" So much for not speaking to him.

"Oh, this hour, I'm an aide at the counselor's office. So I'm pretty much free to roam the halls."

I nodded. That made sense.

His eyes searched mine, and I glanced away. "Ellyn, are you okay? Did something happen?"

Just my overly sensitive heart being ripped to shreds and pounded on for no practical reason at all. *We're just friends. That's all we are. It's all we'll ever be. Friends. The end.* Then I said the last thing I could ever imagine saying. "I met Loni Steele today."

He blanched—as in, he literally went white before my eyes. "Y—you did?"

He didn't have to look so dang guilty. "Yep." I took a deep breath. "I'm sure she's nice. I really don't know—we haven't talked much. But I'm sure she is, if you're her boyfriend and all."

At least Zane had the decency to lower his head and look remorseful. He ran one hand through his hair. Then those hazel eyes glued themselves to mine. "You must hate me."

"Why?" I shrugged. "We're just friends, right?" It took every ounce of my self-control to stand there through this awkwardness. Everything I had.

He shook his head as if to say no, and my heart suddenly began to beat again. Just a tiny bit.

"If I'd known I'd meet you … If I'd had any idea a year ago, maybe this would be different right now."

"A year ago?" What did he mean?

"She's had a thing for me for years. We've been friends forever, and in classes together as long as I can remember. So when she brought it up one night, I thought, what the heck? Sure. I was angry at my dad at the time, and it seemed like the perfect way to get back at him. A secret girlfriend. He couldn't tell me what to do. I'd just …" His voice trailed off. "Look, I'm really sorry."

My elbow was itching like crazy. I had to play this cool. "For what?"

"For hurting you."

"Who says you've hurt me?"

He wasn't buying it. The dork didn't believe for a second that I wasn't into him. How was he able to read me so well? "Ellyn?"

"Yes?" I put my hand up. "Look, it's no big deal, okay? We're friends, yes?"

Those eyes of his tugged at my heartstrings. "Please?"

"Of course. And a friendship is all I could imagine or hope for anyway. So don't worry about it."

"But if I ever came across like I was a liar or something the last day or so, just know that I wasn't. Not one part of me was a lie around you. You do fascinate me. You're amazing. You're—"

"Not your girlfriend," I reminded him gently. "Now, stop. This is silly."

He looked like he was going to say something, then changed his mind. "You're right. I hate it, but you're right. I'm not the cheating kind. And Loni loves me, and I'm talking too much as it is. So I'm just going to walk back into the office, and we'll pretend this conversation never happened."

"Okay."

"Ever." He was still looking at me.

I didn't think my chest could take much more. "Okay."

Suddenly, he took my hand. "But if anything changes, can we start again?"

Gah! Don't give me hope. I couldn't handle the stress of hoping something awful would happen to him and Loni. "I don't do 'ifs.' I can't do them. I wouldn't be able to think of anything else."

He nodded. "Why do you have to be so amazing?"

I had to laugh. "You don't even know me. Who's to say that after a week with me, you wouldn't be looking at the next girl anyway? I could be the most annoying person on the planet, for all you know."

Zane leaned forward, placed a very unexpected kiss on my cheek, and whispered, "I doubt it. I've never felt this way before, and I can't imagine ever feeling this way again." Then he turned around and walked into the office without another word.

For the first time in my life, my knees completely turned to jelly. Everything Maralyn had ever said about romantical things all came bounding back into my memory—and yet nothing seemed to replace the words Zane had just said to me.

Those had to have been the most perfect words ever spoken. After a few minutes of quiet reflection—where my mind was anything but quiet, racing through each and every part of the conversation—I finally decided that now would be a good time to go to class.

I was floating. It honestly felt like my shoes weren't touching the floor. How was this possible?

But as I opened the door to chemistry, the reality of everything that had just happened hit me like a backpack full of books. The one guy I'd set my hopes on was already taken. Why did I have such awful luck? And how was I supposed to keep this secret from my family? They were so excited for me. I couldn't move.

Thirty kids turned in their seats to stare at me.

I shut the door again.

The teacher came out into the hall and commented that I didn't look so great and should probably head to the office. But I couldn't. Not yet. I needed a few minutes to myself. "Give me a little bit," I said.

"Really—you can't just stand here in the hall. It's against school policy. You either need to be in class or go to the office and call your parents."

My parents? There was just one. *Parent.* I wished Dad was there right now. I wished he was telling me what to do and making it all better—and also telling me what a jerk Zane was. Because he would, and just that small thought could've made this whole day better. But Dad wasn't there.

And I was alone. Again. Like always. Just like I knew I would be.

As soon as I began to shake, the teacher stopped waiting for me to compose myself. Instead, he wrapped an arm around me and sort of pushed-walked me toward the office himself.

Back toward the one place I really didn't want to be.

Headed straight for Zane again.

NINE
♥
SURPRISE ENCOUNTER

I purposely looked away from the open door of the counselor's office as the teacher and I headed toward the main desk.

"Miss Dashwood isn't feeling very well," the teacher said as we approached the large countertop. "Can you talk with her and see if she needs to go home?"

Could he speak any louder?

"Of course." The woman behind the counter smiled as she approached us. "What's wrong, dear?"

"I'm going back to my class." The chemistry teacher nodded and left the room before I could say anything.

Once he was gone, the lady asked again, "What's wrong? Are you not feeling well?"

I glanced toward the counselor's office and didn't see Zane. "I'm not sure."

"Well, are you sick?"

"No. Not really. I really would rather not go to class, though. I don't think I could handle it."

"Aren't you one of the new girls?"

"Yes, my sister and I enrolled yesterday."

"That's right." She grinned. "You're Ellyn Dashwood?"

"Yes."

She rummaged through a file of papers and pulled one out. She examined it for a minute and then seemed satisfied. "Well, it says here that as long as a parent has been notified, you're free to leave campus if for any reason, you don't feel well enough to attend school. Would you like us to call your mom and let her know?"

I had no idea. "So I have a 'get out of jail free' card?"

"Pretty much." She chuckled. "I wish I had one of these when I was younger."

I still didn't get it. "But why?"

She looked back down at the paper in her hand. "It says here that it's for medical reasons. Something your mom asked to implement due to a recent tragic event in your family."

Ah, yeah. My autism . . . and Dad. How could I have forgotten? I thought about leaving, but what would be better? Hiding at home and being away from school? Or actually sticking it out and facing the worst of it? As fun as it sounded to stay at school and face junk, I took the easy route. "Yes, I'd like to talk to my mom and go home." Already, my breathing was getting weird again, just thinking of staying.

Within seconds, the lady was calling my mom. Before I knew it, I was getting my stuff from my locker and heading out the main entrance of the school. The secretary even offered to send a note to my sister to let her know I'd gone home early.

As soon as I made it outside, I could feel the stress leaving. Wow. How had I not known this was an option before? Had it always been on my records that I could ditch school?

As I headed toward the parking lot, the tension continued to leave. I'd just reached the sidewalk when I heard a shout behind me.

"Maralyn!"

I turned to see if my sister was out here, but saw a sandy-haired guy I didn't know running toward me. "Maralyn!" he called again. "Wait."

I sighed and waited for him to catch up. My elbow itched. This was the hardest part about being a twin—people thinking you were someone else.

He began to talk before I could set him straight. "Hey, I saw you from the window." He pointed to the side of the building and then smiled as he approached. "Here. You left your stuff in the music room yesterday." He handed me a pile of piano books. "You're leaving early? I hope you're not sick."

I stared at the books for about three seconds before it dawned on me what was happening. Mara must have been playing the piano at school, but I had no idea she still held on to her old books. Since we'd sold the piano to move here, I'd assumed she'd gotten rid of them. "Thank you, but they're not mine. I'm Ellyn, Maralyn's twin sister."

"Oh!" His tanned face went a bit redder. "I'm so sorry. I should've known you weren't her."

My eyebrows rose, and I tried to hide the grin attempting to pop out. "Yeah, no worries. People get us confused all the time."

"Well, hey. I'm Skyler Brandon. I guess I should probably introduce myself, especially if I'm gonna chase after you and all."

"Hi." His smile was contagious. "So, do you take a music class with my sister?"

"Uh, no. I'm actually the student teacher—the aide for Ms. Billington, the choir director. I come here and work kind of like an intern while I get my teaching degree. Maralyn came in during lunch yesterday and used the piano, but forgot her books when she went to class."

There was a lot to process. Suddenly, I needed to breathe again. Focus. *Answer him about Mara playing the piano.* "I had no idea."

"She's crazy good. Probably one of the best pianists I've heard in forever."

I looked at him funny. I knew she had a way of attracting guys, but come on. This college guy couldn't have become her fan too. "You really think she's good?"

He let out a puff of air. "Yeah, I'm sure she could get into Juilliard if she wanted."

"What?" I forgot everything else. "Juilliard? Seriously?"

He shrugged. "Why not? She must have the piano going twenty-four/seven at home."

"Actually, we don't have a piano anymore."

"Wow. She reminds me of a girl who lived in Farmington a couple of years ago, a prodigy. Amanda Ellis. Have you heard of her? She's really good. Even has a CD out now."

"Prodigy? You think Maralyn is *that* good?"

"I don't know. I only heard her once. But I was impressed."

Judging by that bashful look, he was probably more impressed with her smile than her playing. Mara loved to play the piano—maybe she *was* a prodigy—but chances were, Skyler was a little smitten. Then again, who *wasn't* smitten by her?

Wait a minute. Was he the one she was talking about in the hall? No. That guy was named Harrison, and she just met him today. I looked Skyler over closely. He wasn't the hottest guy I'd ever seen, but he wasn't bad-looking, either. Kind of one of those nice, normal guys. His green eyes were pretty cool. I'd never seen green that color before—almost like a light lime color or something. "Hey, you have a brown spot in your left eye. That's cool."

Skyler's eyebrows rose. I realized I probably looked like a dork, staring at him. He handled it okay, though, as he pointed to his eye. "Yeah, I'm blind in this one. The one with the brown speck."

"Are you really?"

"Yeah." He grinned. "It didn't stop me from doing everything I've wanted to do, though. My parents were worried when I was little, but I've never known any different, so it's just me."

All of a sudden, my curiosity kicked in. "Do you mean sports?"

"Yep. Everything. Football, basketball, swim team. I also love kayaking, rappelling, mountain climbing …all of it."

"So, what made you go into teaching?"

He shrugged. "My love of music, I guess. I've always been a big fan. I play a couple of instruments myself and dabbled in choirs and things over the years. And I think I can make a difference, so here I am."

How was this guy so awesome?

He coughed and then looked around. "Hey, sorry. I didn't mean to stop you. Anyway, when you see Maralyn, let her know I said hi."

"How old are you?" I blurted out before I'd thought it through. I quickly tried to cover it up. "You look pretty young."

He stepped back and scratched his jaw before answering. "I'll be twenty this summer."

"Nineteen!" I was surprised. "Aren't you way too young to be an aide?"

He dipped his head. "Technically, yes. But my dad's on the Bloomfield school board, and I used to go to this school. Ms. Billington needed someone this year because the band teacher had maternity leave, so Ms. Billington is filling in double duty between band and choir. My dad pulled some strings. I'm now doing online courses from NMSU and I'm up here helping out. I'm volunteering, so it's not like I'm a real teacher, just an aide—but without as many restrictions."

Um, I wasn't quite sure I'd caught all of that. But I'd definitely caught enough to be impressed. "Wow."

"Well, I've got to go back in." He headed back a few more steps and sort of gave me a salute. "Tell Maralyn I said hi."

"Thanks. I will."

I smiled as I turned around and crossed through the fence onto the sidewalk. It was obvious he was completely into Maralyn. He'd be perfect for her, if she'd give him a chance. Sighing, I looked both ways before crossing the road. The fact that she hadn't mentioned him meant that she probably didn't care. Which was a bummer. So, he wasn't the cutest guy, but he was definitely more interesting than the typical popular guys she usually brought home.

It didn't matter. At least *she* had choices.

I unlocked the door and walked into the house. Making my way into my room, I dropped the piano books and my bag on the floor and collapsed into the comfy chair next to the bed. I looked around and tried hard not to imagine the large home we'd come from, or the beautiful things we used to have—like Maralyn's grand piano. It made me a bit sad to remember the way things used to be, but it didn't matter. All that wealth was nothing more than stuff anyway. Without Dad, it was pointless.

Thinking about how much Dad had loved to hear Mara play, my mind began to wander, and I thought of all the attention Mara got and all the friends and talents she had. I wasn't jealous, actually, though I probably could've been if I wanted to be. Fact was, for as outgoing and flamboyant as she was, she was still kind. She still cared about others, and she was genuinely talented.

But as my dad pointed out so often it stuck, I could do marvelous things she'd never imagine. We were both unique, and there was so much to celebrate because of it. I would never be attracted to her boyfriends anyway—at least, not like how I thought of Zane. Which was a stupid thought to have.

Why hadn't he just told me about Loni? Why had this been a weird drama moment? I can't handle those things. I need quiet and stress-free zones, and not the craziness of girlfriends and hurt feelings and all that stupidity.

I didn't want him to hurt Loni, either. In fact, if he'd broken up with her because of me, I'd honestly never speak to him again. That kind of disloyalty wasn't going to work with me. I needed security. I needed an anchor. I couldn't handle flimsy feelings. And if he'd actually break up with his girlfriend over *one day* with me, then who's to say he wouldn't break up with me after the next girl came along? Oh, no—I couldn't handle that. I would constantly feel inferior to anyone he spoke with, wondering if he'd fall for her as quickly as he'd claimed to with me.

No. This was better. If, after a few months down the road,

they still weren't getting along and eventually broke up and then he came back, then *maybe* I'd consider him. Until then, he was taken, and I had to deal with it.

I must've fallen asleep. The next thing I heard was a loud banging on the front door. I glanced at the clock and saw that it was almost three. School was already over. I heard the banging again, followed by the doorbell. "Ellyn, hurry and open up!" It was Maralyn. Her voice didn't sound natural at all. Something was wrong.

A shot of fear coursed through me. I ran into the living room and opened the door. A tall, dark-haired guy stood there, holding Maralyn in his arms. They both looked stressed.

My heart leaped to my throat. "W—what happened?" I asked as I moved out of the way to let them in.

"It's just a sprained ankle." He carried her past me and into the living room.

"I'm okay." Maralyn grimaced. "Just set me down on the couch."

"Do you need me to call Mom? The doctor?" I had no idea what to do, and my brain went completely blank.

She winced as he sat her down. "Yeah, someone better call Mom. I was a major klutz and tried to—ouch!"

"Sorry. Are you okay?" the guy asked her.

Maralyn nodded, but didn't finish her story, so he did.

"She tried to chase some papers into the road, but fell right in the middle of the street. The worst part was that she'd been so worried about the papers, she hadn't looked where she was going, and a car nearly hit her."

I gasped. I don't think I could've spoken if I wanted to.

"Harrison saved me." Maralyn smiled. "He was this amazing knight in shining armor."

He looked a bit freaked out, like it was more serious than she was letting on. "I decided I'd better get her off the road before another car had to swerve around her. So here we are."

TEN

BLACK KNIGHT

"I'm fine, Ellyn," Maralyn said. "I can see it on your face already—you're beginning to panic. Don't. Sit with me and I'll show you—it's just a twisted ankle, no big deal."

"How do you know it's not broken?" Harrison asked. "You don't."

She rolled her eyes. "I've sprained my ankle a hundred times. It's fine."

Mara did have a habit of hurting herself, but I needed to be sure. One of us should talk to Mom, too. "Where's your phone?"

She reached into her back pocket and pulled it out. I quickly dialed Mom's number, and then after trying to explain, I handed the phone over to Mara. While she talked, I stared at the guy who'd sat down on the overstuffed chair next to her.

So this was her dream guy? He looked like a model. I had no idea what to say to him.

I was silent for a little bit until he asked, "So, are you two twins or something?"

"Yep." Sometimes I wondered about people's mental capacities when they asked such blatantly obvious questions.

"Cool." He nodded his head. "I always wanted a twin."

Here it comes. Everyone wanted to be a twin so they could switch and pretend to be each other. Harrison didn't fail.

"Just so he and I could switch classes and no one would know."

"Yeah."

"So, do you guys do that?" he asked.

"No."

The room went quiet—well, at least we did. Mara was still talking to Mom.

I glanced around, not quite ready to make eye contact again. It took a minute before I realized I was probably being very rude. "Do you need something? Water? Or are you hungry?"

He grinned, and I nearly swooned. Okay, he wasn't my type, but I could see why Maralyn was into him. "Nah, I'm okay. I'm just worried about your sister. Hope you guys don't mind if I hang for a little while until I know she's fine?"

He was definitely like a knight. Or one of those characters you read about in books. "Sure."

Maralyn hung up the phone. "Mom says she's on her way now." She rolled her eyes. "I can't believe all the attention one little sprained ankle gets me."

"How does it feel?" he asked.

She lay back on the couch and propped her foot on the armrest. "Better. Hurts, but better." Then she smiled at him dazzlingly. "Thank you so much. I really can't repay you for this."

"It was my pleasure." His eyes never left hers.

For the first time since they arrived, I felt like a third wheel. I coughed softly. "So, how did you guys meet?"

"He was so sweet. As we were walking out of school, I dropped my essay notes right in front of him. They flew everywhere, and he stopped to help me get them back."

"Of course, that's when she fell. I picked her up, and we got to know each other as I carried her all the way here." They both laughed. Why did I have a suspicious feeling about the papers falling right in front of him? I could never understand the lengths Maralyn would go to just to get some guy's attention. It was embarrassing.

But it worked. She always knew just how to snag the exact guy she wanted. *Now, let's hope Harrison turns out to be someone worthy of her.*

By the time my mom pulled up, they'd been discussing their favorite movies for at least ten minutes. Surprisingly, Harrison didn't just know all of the musicals that were Maralyn's favorite, but he could quote them, too.

"Oh, my gosh!" Mom said as she burst into the door. "Thank you so much for saving my daughter, Harrison! You're wonderful." She ran over to Maralyn and knelt down on the large red rug in front of her. "Now, tell me everything. How's it feeling? Are you okay? Have you tried walking on it? Should we go see a doctor?"

Katelyn closed the front door and walked over to me. "What happened? Did she really trip in the street?"

"Yep. And Harrison saved her." I pointed to him.

He waved over at us from the overstuffed chair next to Maralyn.

It took only a second or two before Katelyn scampered over to him and began to ask all sorts of questions, enough to keep them both occupied while Mom decided if Mara's injury was serious or not.

I'd stood up when Mom came in the room and had been standing next to the wall, quite uncomfortably, not sure how to help or what to do. Mom turned to me. "Ellie, get our guest something to drink and bring some juice for Mara, just in case she goes into shock."

Shock? If she was going to go into shock, it would've happened by now, wouldn't it? She sprained her ankle over thirty minutes ago. Probably more like forty. I tried to think back on the first responder course Mom had made me and Mara take last summer. Maybe I'd forgotten something. I shrugged and then headed into the kitchen.

All must've been well because when I came back with glasses of orange juice for Harrison and Maralyn, the whole group was laughing.

Mom waved me in. "Come and listen. Harrison is sharing all the silly things about living in this small town."

"Do you know anything about New Mexico?" he asked me. I shook my head. "Not really."

He grinned and leaned forward with his elbows on his knees. His smiled included us all. "Okay. So you know how at Mexican restaurants, the green sauce is the mild one? Well, not here. If you order the green, remember that you can never go back. It'll feel like your mouth is on fire, but you won't be able to stop eating it. It's that good."

I looked at him like he was crazy. "There's no way I'd keep eating something that was too spicy."

His confidence only grew. "Ah, you say that now, but

you've never tasted New Mexican green chile. You have no idea how amazing that stuff is. None."

Maralyn laughed. "Oh, I doubt you'll ever be able to convince Ellyn to try it. She doesn't do spicy at all."

He clutched his heart and fell back on the couch. "I can't handle this! Make it stop. You live in New Mexico, and you can't take the heat! Ahh!" He immediately popped back up again and reached over, clasping Maralyn's hand. "Tell me this horror stops with your sister. Tell me this same unspicy gene has not crossed over to you, too."

Good grief. With drama like this, who needed TV? I shook my head.

Mara giggled and swatted him. "You're safe. I love spicy food."

He waggled his brows. "Perfect." Then he leaned toward her. "So, tell me what else you like."

Katelyn sat down on the couch next to me. "She loves boyfriends! A lot of boyfriends!"

Mom and Mara gasped, but I admit it, I totally laughed. I couldn't help it. "It's true."

"Katelyn and Ellyn, you can both leave the room if you're going to act this way!" Mom was completely horrified.

But Harrison was all ears. "Really? You like a lot of boyfriends? All at the same time, or what?"

I smirked. "She's had more than one."

Mom gave me a "get out" look.

I snatched Katelyn's hand and stood up.

Maralyn was blushing. "Not at the same time." She brushed her hair back from her face and positioned herself more comfortably on the couch. "But yes," she admitted. "I've had a few boyfriends."

"I'll bet you have." Harrison's answering grin almost looked like a leer from where I stood.

Katelyn pulled on my hand. "Why do I have to go too? I want to stay here and meet Mara's new boyfriend."

Mom cleared her throat and fake laughed. "Go, both of you." Her words had an edge of unmistakable steel in them. "Why don't you start dinner? Now."

"What should I make?" I asked as I pulled Katelyn toward the doorway.

"Anything. I don't care. Just get something started so we don't starve." *And neither of you embarrass us again.* She didn't have to say the last part—her look spoke volumes.

I couldn't help it—my smile grew. I should've felt ashamed for laughing, but I just couldn't. Katelyn was too funny for words, and it was so true!

As we headed into the kitchen, I could hear Mom inviting Harrison to stay for dinner. I opened the nearest cupboard to get inspiration and sighed. Hopefully, I could manage to get through this night without completely losing it. I mean, I'm sure Harrison was great and all, but something about him didn't sit quite right with me. Maybe he was a little too perfect. I never had trusted perfect people. They seemed to be the first to let you down when things got messy.

I opened another cupboard and found some spaghetti noodles. Exactly the type of meal I was hoping to make—something quick, painless, and easy. In the adjoining shelf, I found a large can of marinara sauce. Voila! Now I just needed to find the ingredients to make garlic bread, and dinner would be done before I knew it.

"Grab the big pot under the stove and fill it with water from the sink," I said to Katelyn. "I'm gonna start on mixing together some yummy garlic sauce to go over the bread."

"Mmm…" She was already licking her lips. "Can I help with dessert? I think we should have brownies to celebrate Maralyn's new boyfriend."

"He's not her boyfriend yet."

"Yet." Katelyn pulled out the pot and began to fill it with water. "But I bet you he is by tonight."

I shook my head. "I don't think Maralyn is that rash. No girl should be. She usually waits a couple of weeks. You should definitely get to know someone before you commit to them."

"What does 'rash' mean?" She carried the pot to the stovetop, and I added some salt to it before turning on the burner.

"It means that you're doing something quickly without thinking about it first." I found some sourdough bread in the fridge and pulled out the butter. Then I got the parsley and garlic powder from the spice cabinet.

"I like to think about what I'm doing," Katelyn said in her best older voice. She opened a cupboard and pulled out a nine-by-nine baking pan.

"Hey, could you get me a cookie sheet while you're in there?" I put a cube of butter into a coffee mug and set it in the microwave as she handed over the cookie sheet. "Now, what did you say about thinking?" I asked, completely forgetting what we were talking about for a second. There were just enough slices of bread to cover the metal tray.

She gave me a funny look and put a hand on her hip. "You always forget things, don't you?"

"Yep." I couldn't deny it if I tried. "Sorry. I don't mean to."

She shrugged and then walked over to the small pantry closet near the counter. It took two whole seconds for her to pop back out with a box of brownie mix and a smile on her face. "I was saying how I plan to think about what I'm doing." Her smile turned into a smug grin. "Like these brownies. It's not hard to follow the pictures on the back of the box. I can get all the stuff, and then you can tell me how much to put in. See? I'm thinking about what I'm doing."

"Ah … Yes, you're not being rash at all." I stifled a grin and then pulled the melted butter from the microwave. *She really is an adorable little sister*, I thought as I mixed in a few dashes of garlic powder and parsley into the mug of melted butter. Then stirring with a pastry brush, I began to slather the mixture onto the sourdough bread. A minute or so later, I was placing the tray into the oven and setting the timer for fifteen minutes.

The water still hadn't started to boil, so I walked over and helped Katelyn with the brownies. She'd collected two eggs, a bottle of vegetable oil, and a cup of water. "Wow. You really can figure out these boxes! Good job." I would've given her a hug, but then thought better of it. I really didn't like hugs, so she might not like them either. For an awkward moment, we just stared at each other, and then I lightly patted her head.

She laughed. "You're so funny sometimes."

At least she thought I was funny. "Thanks."

Everyone in the other room roared with hilarity at that exact second. My heart clenched. It wasn't until Harrison began to talk loudly that I realized they were laughing about something he was telling them and not at me. Right. "Well, let's get busy. We've still got some more to do."

ELEVEN
♥
STOP THIS TRAIN!

Mom had us all eat in the living room so Mara didn't have to get up. After Harrison left, I finally remembered the music books and placed them on Mara's lap. "A student teacher named Skyler brought these to me. He thought I was you at first. I guess you left them in the music room yesterday."

"Oh." She didn't seem that impressed. "Dang it. I was hoping I could keep them there instead of hauling them to and from school every other day."

Every other day? "Are you practicing for something?"

"No." She sighed. "I just miss playing and didn't want to make Mom feel bad."

I looked toward the doorway. Mom and Katelyn were still in the kitchen doing the dishes. "Probably smart. She'd be upset if she knew how much you wanted your piano back."

"It is what it is. Not like we can change anything."

I sat down on the chair where Harrison had been. "Well,

Skyler says you're really good. Like, Juilliard good. He said he thought you were a prodigy."

"Really?" She seemed surprised.

"I think he likes you."

She looked away. "Ew. Don't say that. He's thirty or something."

I laughed. "More like nineteen, but whatever. It's clear you're not into him, so it's better not to give the poor guy anything to hope for."

"Yeah, nerdy musicians aren't really my type." She shuddered.

I swear, sometimes my sister could be a snob and not even know it. "What does that mean?"

"Nothing." She raised her brows. "He's just not my type, okay?"

I looked at her without saying anything. Fine. She was a big girl—she could choose who she wanted to hang out with. But honestly, in my opinion, she needed someone just like Skyler. He was helpful, kind, caring, smart—and most importantly—normal, not one these total uber popular guys she usually fell head over heels for.

"Besides, why would I look at some student teacher when Harrison goes to the same school?" She grinned and plopped her head on the pillow. "Harrison is everything a guy should be. Heroic, funny, intelligent, sweet, and hotter than a New Mexican chile."

I chuckled. "You don't even know what one tastes like!"

"I'll find out. He's already promised to take me to three of his favorite Mexican restaurants and then let me decide which one we'll always go to after that."

"Always?" My eyebrows rose. "As in, forever?"

She bit her lip. "Does it matter? Sure, if he's paying. I have no problem going to any and every restaurant where he's willing to take me."

"Just how many dates did you two set up tonight? Aren't these things better planned one at a time?" Good grief, nothing like throwing caution to the wind.

"Why would we wait? He has about twenty different places he says he's excited to show me. What's wrong with planning them all?"

"Twenty! Are you kidding me?" How was that even possible? She had to be the only girl on the planet who could get a guy to commit to take her out to so many places within two or three hours after meeting her.

"He likes me, just like I said he would. What's the big deal?"

"Don't you think that's a bit unsafe? I mean, we don't even know the guy. He could be a serial killer or something."

Maralyn didn't even laugh. In fact, she looked down right mad. "Why would you even say something like that?" Her voice rose. "You don't know the guy, and you're already accusing him of being some—ugh!" She threw her hands in the air. "Before I've even gone on a date with him!"

"I'm only saying, let's wait a minute to see what he's like first."

"I don't have to wait. I already know what he's like. Ten minutes next to him, and I knew he was amazing."

"What's going on in here, girls?" Mom came into the room with a wet towel in her hand.

"Ellyn's just jealous because she's never had a real boyfriend, and so she's trying to interfere with Harrison."

Mom looked surprised. "What?"

Nice. "Well, thanks, Maralyn." I stood up. "I can't take this. I'm leaving." I walked to the doorway and then turned around. "And for the record, I'm not jealous. I'm worried about my sister. Trusting a guy we've only met once and planning several dates with him, as if they were already together, before she's even been out with him, didn't sound very safe. But maybe I'm wrong. Either way, it doesn't matter. I hope you're right, Maralyn. I hope he's awesome."

My heart became heavier with each step I took as I headed to the bedroom. As soon as the door was locked, I plopped down on my bed and reminded myself of several reasons why I shouldn't get emotional right now. There was no reason to be hurt when technically, I was the one who crossed the boundaries first.

Why shouldn't I let her be happy and assume everything was perfect with Harrison? What did it matter, anyway? And she didn't know that Zane already had a girlfriend. She had no idea how badly she was slicing me with her words.

Maybe Maralyn was right—maybe I was jealous. Maybe now, after finally understanding what it felt like to have my heart somersault in my chest because of a guy—maybe, just maybe, I was a little bummed I wouldn't ever feel that again.

I stared at the wooden slats above me. Life was ridiculous. I was pretty sure it wasn't meant to be this hard. I sighed and rolled over. Perhaps now was a good time to do my homework, or read, or practice being normal so more people liked me.

I wanted to cry. I really did, but I wouldn't let myself. There were times when if I concentrated hard enough, I could actually stop the hysteria, or emotional block, or daydream from happening. It'd taken years and years of practice, but

I'd been mastering it slowly.

I used to burst out in random giggles or start speaking out loud when I'd daydream—especially when I was younger. It's what made the other kids laugh at me the most. There we'd all be, listening to the teacher, and I'd hear a word or two about something or another, and off I'd go on my own adventure. Before I knew it, my mind would wander to far-off places and I'd be living in that world, truly, completely living in it. I couldn't hear anything but what was going on in that realm until someone touched me and I'd blink back to reality once more.

Usually, I'd be so jolted, it was almost terrifying to find myself someplace way different from where I'd just been. And not only so different, but calm, and normal, with lots of people staring at me. I hated it when that happened. It was frightening, but it was also annoying, like being woken up in the middle of an amazing dream. I wanted to go back, but I couldn't.

It's probably why I loved reading so much. If I went to magical far-off lands in a book, people were happy about it and encouraged it. So, as I read, it wouldn't matter if I giggled out loud or told off a certain character—none of it mattered because I was reading, so I had an excuse.

Yes, I do feel this world is a little bit messed up. And who would really want to live here when they could be several thousand miles away in their own minds? I grinned at my joke and then wished Dad were here so I could share the thought with him. He would get it. He would understand.

I then thought about Zane. I was pretty sure he would understand me too, or at the very least, try to understand why it was so much easier to leave reality. When you were mentally gone, you were safe, free. You had no hard choices to make, or hurtful sisters to argue with.

I pulled away from that thought and sat up in my bed. Time to come back to reality again. Besides, I was pretty sure I had homework to do. Dragging my backpack over to me, I got out my notebook and laptop and went to work. Enough was enough—no matter how much I struggled with autism, my teachers really didn't like it when I forgot to turn in my work.

Time to make them happy. At least somebody would be.

{♥}

Maralyn didn't make it to school the next day, or the day after that. Since the swelling got so bad overnight, Mom took her to the doctor the morning after she got hurt, and he recommended that she stay off it for a couple more days. When she didn't show up to school people began to get worried.

I could hardly make it out of the school building after the final bell before the masses began to inquire.

"Hey, Ellyn!" Skyler jogged toward me, weaving through students in the crowded hallway just as I opened the main doors to walk out.

I held the door for him. "What's up?"

He stepped into the sunshine and then moved us both a few paces away. "I heard Maralyn got hurt. Is she okay?"

"Yeah, she just sprained her ankle. Doc said to keep off it until tomorrow."

He looked relieved. "I was worried when she didn't show up again today that something worse might be going on."

"Nope. Just her ankle. She's in a lot of pain, though."

"Wow. I hope she gets better soon."

"Thanks." I smiled. Skyler really was a sweetheart. "I'll let her know you wish her well."

Just then, Loni burst out the doors and down the few steps toward us. "Ellyn! Are you going home right now?" Hello? Couldn't she see I was already in the middle of a conversation?

"Yes," I answered shortly as I turned my attention back to Skyler. Hopefully, she'd get the hint.

She didn't. "Good!" She grinned. "Can I walk with you? I've got a card for Maralyn."

I didn't even know they knew each other. And now she was going to find out where I lived. Nice. How could I get out of this? I sighed. "Sure."

"Oh, do you mind if I tag along too?" Skyler's face went bright red when I turned toward him.

"What did you say?"

He ducked his head and looked up at me. "I'm assuming she's bored out of her mind and would like some company. Just asking if I could come."

What could it hurt? Maybe he'd be able to buffer Loni. "I'm sure it's no big deal. Come on."

It really wasn't that big of a deal. My mom would be fine with people coming to cheer her daughter up. Loni and Skyler carried the bulk of the conversation as we made the short trek together. He prattled on about teaching and how rough it can be while Loni spent the whole time dropping hints about how hard it is to be single, but unable to date.

Each time she did, I felt stabbed, and Skyler became a bit more leery of her. To a guy, I could see how that would come across like she was hitting on him, which was strangely a lot funnier than the truth.

As we went in the house, everything seemed to be going great. Maralyn was pleasantly surprised to have company—and loved having more listeners for the story of her twisted ankle. She was a good halfway through when the doorbell rang.

I left the little group and answered it.

There on the porch was Zane.

What in the world was he doing here? And how was I going to explain him to Loni?

TWELVE
♥
SPEAK OF THE DEVIL

"Zane!" I gasped.

"I'm sorry. Is this a bad time? I was hoping to speak with you."

I glanced behind me. No one had stepped out of the living room. "I—yeah, now is kind of bad," I whispered.

He gently tugged on my hand and pulled me out the door. "Just for a few minutes, and then I promise to leave."

"Okay," I grumbled as I shut the front door. Maybe no one heard me answer it. My heart was beating too fast to think properly, and I was curious to find out what he wanted.

"Are you guys having a party or something?" he asked.

"No. A couple of people came to see my sister, who sprained her ankle. What do you need?"

"I just—I feel really bad for how things came off the other day. And I wanted to see how you were, and . . ." He ran his fingers through his hair. "I don't know. Make sure we're chill and still friends."

"Friends?" My eyebrows rose.

"Yeah. I just miss y—"

The front door opened, and Loni peeked her head out. "Ellyn, who are you—Zane! What are you doing here?" She moved onto the front step and looked suspiciously between the two of us.

I wanted to die. "He'd heard you were here and came by to see you," I lied. It was stupid, I know. It really was. I should've just told her that he came to see me, but I couldn't. I didn't want to create even more drama.

Zane, on the other hand, wasn't taking it. "I'm sorry to hear Maralyn isn't feeling well, but I actually was hoping to talk to Ellyn for a minute. To make sure we're still okay."

"What do you mean?" Loni asked.

I needed to put my hand to my face. "Nothing. He just wanted to make sure we're still friends." I looked up to him for reassurance.

"Yep." His eyes met mine. "Are we?"

Oh, good grief. Why was he making a big deal out of this?

"So, you guys are planning on being all chummy, then?" Her hands went to her hips, and she smirked. It wasn't a good look on her, but I didn't say anything.

"I don't know." His gaze connected with mine again. "If I'm lucky. But Ellyn will need to decide that."

Would it be awful to say I felt like I was somewhere far away and dreaming the words coming out of his mouth? That I craved this sort of friendship with this guy more than I did air? I needed someone to understand me and bring me the balance he seemed to bring. Would that be awful? Because I felt it. I felt every single bit of that. I was awful. I knew I was awful. My elbow itched, and I couldn't think straight. And I missed him.

I took a deep breath.

Zane's eyes never left mine. "Loni, could you give us just a few more minutes?"

I didn't dare look at her. I could tell she was torqued by the way the door slammed as she went back in.

He closed his eyes and winced. "I've probably done the stupidest thing I could do, huh?"

"It was kind of rude."

"Was it?" He looked at me again.

My heart was in my throat. "Yeah."

"I'll apologize and take her out tonight and try to explain this to her."

"Explain what?" Seriously, I had no idea what this was.

He seemed lost. "I don't know. All I know is that I think about you and worry about you and wonder what's happening in your world. And hoping those around you are nice and that you're fitting in—and mostly, I can't sleep knowing I've hurt you."

My breathing became more erratic. "This isn't helping, though."

"Isn't it?"

"No."

"Not even a little bit?"

Maybe. "No."

"But why?"

"Because every time I talk to you, I feel guilty because you've got a super-angry girlfriend."

"She's nice, though … she's not always angry. She'll come around."

"Still isn't helping."

"I know. But why can't we be friends? Why can't we argue

about scientists and theories and rack our brains for cures and . . . where have you been all my life?"

"What?"

"I'm not kidding. Where have you been? I needed you in elementary and middle school and the last three years at this high school. No one else thinks like you do. I feel like I'm going crazy. Like I'm missing out on the greatest opportunity I've ever had just because there are these no boy/girl friend rules when you have a girlfriend. Who makes these things up?"

I had to grin. He was kind of adorable. Then I nodded toward the house. "The angry girlfriends."

"But I'll explain it to her. I'll tell her how there isn't anything between us and how we're just friends and it's crazy to think there's something more than that, right?"

I bit my lip at the look he was giving me. Like he wanted to kiss me right then.

Gah. I couldn't handle this type of drama. "Go away, Zane."

"No."

"Now. Just go." I pointed to his car.

His voice went a bit softer. "No."

My heart sped up a thousand beats a second, and I could hardly breathe. "Yes."

"Do you really want me to?"

No. Never. Stay. "I—uh—yes."

"You hesitated."

I tried not to chuckle. "I have autism. I always hesitate."

"That's because you're smart."

"Maybe."

"If I broke up with her, you'd never talk to me again, would you?"

I shook my head. "No way. Never."

"You value loyalty more than anything."

I nodded. "Loyalty, security, trust ..."

"You're too good, Ellyn Dashwood. And way too good for me."

"Don't say that!" I took a deep breath and decided to be honest. "I like you. I wish we could be friends. I miss you probably way more than you miss me. But I don't see how it'd be possible. I don't like forbidden . . . weirdish things anyway. I like things straight and open. And not silly. And she loves you. Like, really loves you, in a way I wouldn't know about. You guys go way back. Sure, I'm unique, I guess, and new. But I'm not someone you should break a promise for, and if I ever became that girl, I'd never forgive you. My own guilt would fester too much to want to be near you. I need to be free from that stress."

"Did I hurt you?"

"Are you a sadist or something? Why are you so fascinated by if I'm hurt or not?"

"Because I care."

"Well, stop. It's weird."

"No, it's not."

"Yes." I nodded. "It is. Very." I placed a hand on my hip. "Look, I'm just a girl who feels strongly and differently about things. I'm too blunt for my own good, but more than that, I'm not worth the anxiety."

"Please be my friend."

"And do what, Zane?"

"I've told you! Talk about things—discuss—"

"Scientists. Yes, I know. I meant, how? What's your plan?"

"I don't know. I haven't gotten that far. First was to convince you that this is worth a shot."

"You really have no idea what you're doing, do you?"

He broke his composure and laughed. "None at all. Nada. Zilch." He opened his arms wide. "Honestly, this was just an impulse. I drove by your house like three times, up and down the street, and then finally knocked on the door. I haven't practiced any of this."

How could you miss someone who hurt you so much? "Is friendship even possible? We're in high school. I don't think it works the same way in the grown-up world."

He smirked. "Grown-up world?"

"Are you mocking me right now?"

"Yep." His face fell a bit as our eyes locked again. "Tell me what you want, and it's yours. Anything."

You. Not this. But you. Or maybe not you. A friend. Someone who sees me. You. Definitely you. I stared at him forever. I wanted to look away. I fought it so much—but I didn't. Couldn't. After a long time I said quietly, "I think I'd actually like this to work, please."

The relief I saw pour over his face couldn't be real, could it? This was the stuff in books and movies—I was sure of it. The kind of moments you only read about, but never experience.

He nodded and let out a breath. "Okay. Let's figure this out. We're both highly intelligent beings—well, one of us clearly smarter than the other . . ." He winked. "I'm sure we can come up with something."

"I don't know, but we need to hurry so I can get back to my sister, and Loni doesn't—"

His eyes lit up. "My sister. That's it. It's perfect!"

"What is?"

Grabbing my hands, he answered, "We'll be like brother and sister."

"We will?"

"Yeah. I'll just treat you like I would a sister. Forget the friend thing—there's too much of a bond here for that anyway. Let's just jump to family. This could totally work. I'll explain to Loni that I see you as a sister, and everything will be fine."

"Sister?" It took a second, but I was actually okay with that, strangely enough. Any guilt I had went away. "I've always wanted an older brother."

He grinned. "Someone to argue with and protect you and worry about you?"

I smiled back. "Yeah, something like that."

"Good. Then it's settled. From now on, I'm that annoying older brother in your life."

I raised an eyebrow, wondering what I'd gotten myself into. "Nice."

He leaned forward and ruffled my hair with his hand.

Laughing, I pushed him away. "Okay, so maybe not *that* annoying."

Then all of a sudden, he pulled me toward him and crushed me in a huge hug. Every bit of my sensory overload kicked into high gear. I didn't do hugs. They were weird and awkward and a bit miserable. But his large chest wasn't miserable. Maybe the way his arms trapped me was, but resting my cheek against his chest wasn't miserable at all.

"Thank you," he whispered.

It was wonderful to hear and feel his voice as it resonated through him. Slowly, my hands found their way to his back, and that felt kind of amazing too. "You're welcome."

He smelled good as well.

In fact, if I focused on all the really perfect parts of the hug instead of the trapped feeling, I realized I could very easily stay there a few minutes longer.

He pulled away, and I found myself a little lost again. That gaze searched mine once more. "Sorry. I should—I should probably go."

"Yeah." Or heaven knew I'd be back in his arms.

He took another deep breath. "Okay. Then I guess I'll see you at school tomorrow?"

"Sure."

"Right." Zane gave a short little wave before taking a couple of steps back toward his car. "So, thanks again."

Yeah, this was getting weird. How did you say good-bye to your fake brother? "Bye." I guess just like that.

"Bye," he said.

It wasn't until he was almost to the car before we both remembered at the same time.

"Loni!"

He chuckled as he ran past me and opened the door. I let him go inside without me. As the front door closed, I wrapped my arms around myself and watched a car go by. The driver gave a neighborly wave, so I automatically waved back. This Bloomfield living was so much different than anything I'd ever experienced before. Everything was so much friendlier, I guess. It was odd. It was a good odd, though. The New Mexico sunshine peeked brightly from behind a cloud above me. Warmth filled me to my toes. And all at once, I felt there was a bit more happiness than there'd been an hour ago, too. Hope. And possibly—just possibly—new beginnings.

THIRTEEN
♥
THREE'S A CROWD

When I walked back into the house, Loni was saying good-
bye to Maralyn, and Zane was with her—asking Mara
how she was feeling, and talking to Skyler. I stayed in the
background to give them some space.

After they left, I think Maralyn was kind of surprised to
see Skyler chilling out on the couch and chattering away as
if he planned to stay there forever. When he wasn't looking,
she gave me a sort of "save me" face.

I didn't know how she thought I could help. I had no idea
what to do any more than she did. And I also didn't think
having him over for a little longer was all that bad. He was
interesting—we talked about school and his family here in
Bloomfield. It wasn't like he was trying to go all crazy with
political conspiracy theories and stuff. No, he was cool.

But I could tell Maralyn needed something more exciting.
Just when I thought she'd lose it and point him toward the
door, the doorbell rang. I ran to get it.

It was Harrison.

Instantly, her demeanor changed and her face brightened—happiness bubbled from her as soon as she saw me walk in with him. "Harrison! I'm so glad you came. Come in." She sat up straighter and ran her hands through her hair. "What took you so long?"

He walked over and handed her a bouquet of flowers. "Even though these aren't as beautiful as you are, hopefully they can lift your spirits anyway."

She sighed.

He was good. I had to give him credit for that.

And it would seem that Skyler could take a hint. "Well, thank you for putting up with me this long." He nervously grinned as he stood up. He was a little shorter than Harrison. "Glad you've got company to keep you busy. I'll see you around, Maralyn. Hope you feel better soon." He walked to the doorway and turned back, waiting to see if she'd reply.

Harrison sat down on the seat Skyler had vacated, and Maralyn was so lost in Harrison, she didn't even notice that Skyler had been talking to her.

"Maralyn," I said. "Skyler's leaving. Would you like to say good-bye?"

"What?" She glanced over. "Oh. Good-bye." And then her attention and smile were once again turned to Harrison.

"Sorry," I whispered to Skyler as we headed toward the door. My face flushed in embarrassment for him. No one deserved to be treated like that.

He shrugged. "It happens. At least she's excited about something."

I nodded. "Still, I'm sorry. Thanks for coming by. That was sweet of you."

Skyler looked around the little hallway and nodded, not quite meeting my eye. "No problem."

As I opened the door, I decided to step outside and continue chatting to help ease the awkwardness of my sister's sort-of rejection.

"How long have they been going out?" he asked as I closed the door behind us.

"They're not going out. They haven't even been on a date yet."

He seemed surprised. "Then why did he come over?"

"Harrison was there when she twisted her ankle. He rescued her and carried her home."

"Ah. That makes sense."

"Yep."

"Do you think she really likes him?"

What was he asking? I know he saw her face when Harrison came in. "Yes."

He looked toward the road and then squinted out at the sun before meeting my eyes. "So, I guess they'll be together soon?

"I hope not."

His eyebrows rose. "Me neither, but you first. Why don't you want them together?"

"It's not that I don't want them together as much as I don't like the 'soon' part. I think she needs to get to know him first."

"Yes!" He grinned, almost eagerly. "That's it. Make sure she really knows Harrison Crawford before she falls for him. Trust me, she needs to know him first."

My Spidey senses went into overdrive. "Why? What do you mean?" Did he know something we didn't?

"Nothing, really. Just rumors. But nothing." He waved his hand. "I'm sure it's all just gossip anyway."

My heart dropped. It was like waiting for a big reveal on your favorite TV show, the reveal that will most likely ruin what you liked most about that character. Except this wasn't a show—this was real life, and I kind of already had my suspicions. "What have you heard? Tell me. This is my sister we're talking about."

"It's nothing. Seriously. But if I do hear something concrete, I promise to let you guys know." He began to head down the stairs.

"Wimp," I hollered after him.

"What did you call me?" His grin was contagious.

"You heard me."

One eyebrow rose higher than the other. "I see how it is. I tell you you're being smart by hoping your sister won't jump into things, and you call me names."

"Wimp, wimp, wimp."

He walked to his car and then opened the door. "Okay, but give me some time. Let me ask around discreetly and I'll see what I can find out."

"You're going to verify what everybody at school is already talking about?"

He laughed. "No, this isn't the students doing the talking—if it was the students, I'm sure you'd have already heard it. This is the teachers, so it's ten times worse. No, be grateful I'm nice enough to get the facts before sharing all the trash."

Really? Were teachers that bad? I thought you stopped gossiping once you got into the real world. "Fine." I rolled my eyes. "You're a good guy. Happy?"

"Pass that message onto your sister, okay? Looks like I'll need all the help I can get."

I snorted. "Yeah. Um, you try telling my sister anything. If she decides Harrison is the one for her, there's nothing anyone could say to make her see him any differently."

His face grew serious all of a sudden. "That's not good."

I didn't understand why he looked so concerned. "Why?"

He shook his head. "Never mind. I like this saying that goes, 'True character always wins out in the end.' It's so true. I've never met someone who didn't eventually realize the truth of whatever situation I'd find myself in. So if Harrison is a good guy and will take care of her, we'll all see that he's awesome and be done with it. However, if he's not, he won't be able to hide for long. His true character will show through."

"What about yours?"

"Me?" He laughed. "I already know I'm awesome. I'm just banking on the fact that Maralyn will eventually see my true character too." He opened the car door. "Well, I'm off to review my teaching schedule. Glad everything is okay. Bye."

"Bye." I waved as he slipped into his car.

I liked him. I couldn't quite put my finger on why—but I did. There was something about him that was more steady and good than anyone else Maralyn had been interested in. He fit, even if she didn't see it, and I had this huge feeling that he'd always bring out the best in her.

If he got the chance.

As I made my way back into the house, I wondered how I could sneak Skyler into the conversation and get Mara to start thinking about him differently. There were probably several ways to do it, if I could clear my mind enough to think of them.

I walked into the living room and stopped. Harrison and Maralyn were cuddled together on the couch. He sat behind her, his arms wrapped around her waist, and she leaned back against his chest. They were whispering about something, and Mara giggled.

They looked way too cozy.

I backed out of the room and headed to mine. There was no way I'd go in and be the third wheel to their flirting.

By the time Mom made it home, Harrison had been there nearly two hours. I'd walked past the living room twice—once to get a drink, and the other to start dinner. Each time, they looked much more cuddly than the last time. Mom thought it was adorable, so she left them alone to get to know each other better. She also threatened Katelyn to stay far away from them. However, once dinner was ready, I was sent to help Mara hobble to the table with her crutches.

They were out-and-out kissing. Right there in the living room.

Good grief. I cleared my throat, and they guiltily moved apart. "Mom says it's time for dinner." I couldn't even stay in there. I didn't know why, either. I couldn't tell if I was mad at her for not taking things much more slowly, or if I was just weirded out because I caught them kissing. Either way, I could feel myself sort of freaking out. "Harrison, could you help Mara get to the table?"

"Mara, huh?" He grinned.

She playfully swatted at him. "You only get to call me that once you've earned it."

In answer, he kissed her again, right in front of me. I thought I might gag. Something was wrong. Something deeper than my not liking this relationship, but I didn't know what. I just knew I had to get away. Right then.

"Tell Mom I'll be back in a minute."

"What?" Maralyn asked as I stepped out of the room and walked out the front door.

I didn't take time to go back and explain. I just sort of took off. My heart was pounding, my elbow was itching like crazy, and my neck was beginning to sweat. The stress, the timing, the craziness—I don't know what it was. As soon as I hit the sidewalk, I turned left and began to run.

I hadn't actually run away like this since Dad died nearly two months ago. I didn't know where I planned to go, or how far I'd go—I only knew I needed to get away or burst.

A car honked and scared the living daylights out of me. I'd made it to the middle of the road, probably right where Mara had almost gotten hit. Great. Nothing like being the Dashwood dorks who never looked where they were going.

I stumbled out of the way, onto the sidewalk, and bumped into the chain-link fence that wrapped around the school. Everything was confusing. Everything was wrong. And I didn't know why. I followed the fence all the way around until I came to the baseball fields. There were people everywhere, warming up for a game. Ugh. I needed to be alone.

I kept going, wandering along the fence line until I made it to the football field. There were a few people over by the home bleachers, probably the track team finishing up for the day. I slipped into the field area and headed toward the other side of the track, over by the visitor bleachers. Near the side farthest away from anyone was a small tree. I made that my destination and sat down against it.

Sitting where I was, I couldn't even see the field, so I knew I wasn't visible to the team across the way. It was quiet over here. And peaceful.

I wrapped my arms around my legs and rested my head on my knees. What was my problem, anyway? Who cared what Maralyn did or didn't do? She'd had plenty of boyfriends, and she'd always been careful before. Why was it any big deal now? And why in the world was I freaking out just because I watched her kiss someone? Had I really become such a controlling monster that I'd get mad when she didn't do what I wanted her to?

Seriously, what was wrong with me?

I took a deep breath. If I'd just give myself a few minutes, I could usually realize what my real problem was, and then address it. There had to be something much more going on here. But what?

I sighed and then felt a sob catch in my throat. And then another came. And another. No tears—just these weird, almost frustrated cries, or something.

Taking a shaky breath, I willed myself to stop. And then it hit me. Full force, right between the eyes, like a jackknife hitting its mark. I wasn't mad about Mara kissing Harrison. Sure, it irritated me a little, but it didn't freak me out. That wasn't it.

It was Dad.

FOURTEEN
♥
FINDERS KEEPERS

Dad wasn't here. He wasn't here, and it hurt all over again. He wasn't here to protect us from jerky guys, to see if Harrison was good enough, or Skyler, or Zane—or anyone.

He wasn't here to kiss Mom, either. To snuggle with her on the couch, or make her giggle or bring her flowers.

And I was angry that he was gone, that he would leave us when we needed him most, that we had to move away from our house and friends and life and . . . and everything!

And I was upset that Maralyn could so easily slip into a relationship—especially since we'd lost the best man in our lives just a couple of months ago. How could she be ready to move on and be normal?

And everyone else was happy about it.

Everyone except me.

It was like they thought our lives could go back to normal again. Well, guess what? They couldn't. Not now, not ever. Because Dad left us. He was gone. And he wasn't coming back. He wasn't here when we needed him. And he didn't care. I did. I had to do all the caring. I had to worry and wonder and hope—and I hated it. I didn't want to. I wanted *him*! I wanted my dad to be here where he should be.

I hadn't noticed I'd begun to cry until my knees felt wet. Nice. I lifted my head and wiped my eyes.

"Ellyn? You sure make it hard for a guy to stay focused when I keep running into you. Literally."

"Zane?" I opened my eyes and found a pair of very male legs and running shoes in front of me. What were the odds?

He chuckled. "I came over to run a few laps and clear this adorable twin from my head only to find her in the same dang place I came to forget her. How's that for irony?"

I couldn't even think right now. The last thing I wanted was for Zane to witness my pity party. "Yep." That was the best answer I could give. Keeping my head tuned away from him, I tried to be discreet about wiping my face. It didn't work.

"Hey, are you okay?"

When I didn't answer, he sat down next to me.

"What's wrong?"

I shook my head. "Nothing."

"Uh—okay. Would you like to try that again?"

"No."

Suddenly I felt his arm wrap around my shoulders and pull me into him. "Well, if you don't want to tell me, I guess I'll just have to give you some Zane cuddle therapy until you do."

"Zane cuddle therapy?" My voice sounded thick. I was too drained to bother telling him how much I didn't like hugs.

"Yep. It's a real thing. Just wait. You'll feel better in a minute."

I doubted it. It wasn't like he could poof my dad back or something. I grunted in response.

"You're adorable when you grumble like that."

"You're weird."

His arm squeezed me. "You know, I've been called worse."

"You probably have."

We didn't say anything for a few minutes. I guess my grumpiness kept him at bay. It was nice not having to talk.

Then he asked, "So, are you ready to share yet?"

I sighed. "Not really."

"Well, 'not really' is better than 'no.'"

"I need time alone." Why didn't he understand that?

"No. You need a friend."

I needed a dad. "An older brother?"

"That's right. One of those." He scooted in a bit closer. "Well, here I am!"

I chuckled and pushed against him. "Why are you so chipper, anyway?"

"And persistent. You forgot persistent."

"That too. Why?"

"I don't know." His voice got a bit softer. "I must like torture, I guess."

"What do you mean?" I was trying hard not to be curious, but he'd completely thrown me.

He shook his head. "Nope. This isn't about me. This is about you. How can I help?"

"Why are you tortured by being persistent?" I turned around to face him.

Those eyes held mine for a minute, and I saw my own pain mirrored back. "What's wrong?" I asked him.

"What's wrong?" he asked me.

I grinned and turned back around, this time giving in and snuggling into his embrace. "Fine. It's nothing, really. I just miss my dad."

"Ah." He took a deep breath. "I'm sorry."

"Yeah, well … it is what it is."

"It's still hard. And not something you should have to go through alone."

Why was he so . . . so . . . exactly what I needed? "I don't think I want to go through it alone. But I don't know any other way. How do you balance something like death and still live?"

"Well …" He adjusted his position. "I've heard it's amazingly helpful to spend lots of time with older brother-friends who hold you and let you feel as though someone's there."

I couldn't help myself. I gave a small grin. "You have, huh?"

"Yep. It's supposed to be incredibly effective."

I looked out toward the large grassy area.

"And how's it going for you? Better?"

"I don't know. Maybe. Yeah, I guess." I pushed all my thoughts away so I could focus on Zane. "But maybe it's not good."

"Why's that?"

"Because I'm not processing. I'm not working through it. I'm just sitting here with you. Which is nice, don't get me wrong, but I'm not taking time to grieve on my own."

"How many weeks have you already grieved on your own?"

"All of them."

"Exactly. So every now and then, having someone here for you isn't all that bad."

"I hate your logic."

I must've hurt him somehow because he pulled just the slightest bit away. "Yeah, well. I've been told it isn't the best, so you know, maybe I shouldn't be offering advice."

"Okay. So that just flipped. Your mood completely changed. Are *you* ready to talk yet?" When he didn't answer, I nudged him. "What's torturing you?"

Both his arms wrapped around me. "Being here."

"Then why *are* you here?" I tried to pull away, but he held on tighter.

"Hush. Give me a minute, and I'll explain."

Something in his voice made me pause. I really wasn't good with this boy-girl friendship thing. I didn't catch half of what he was trying to convey, but something—something was there. Something I did understand. Longing. He really just wanted to be here with me, but couldn't.

And then it clicked. Heaven help me for being a day late and a dollar short, as my dad would say, but I finally understood his torture. It was my torture too. "You want more than friendship?" I tentatively asked.

"I thought it was obvious."

"I'm not actually Captain Obvious. I'm more like Captain Stup—"

"Stupendous?"

I laughed. "Nerd."

"You know you love my nerdy side."

Love. That word rang around us both for an eon. I couldn't speak if I wanted to.

Thankfully, Zane cleared his throat and changed the subject. "So, tell me about your dad. What triggered the tears?"

"I—I don't know. Maralyn's new boyfriend, I guess."

"Huh?" He pulled away to look at me. "What happened? Do I need to punch someone?"

The look on his face caused me to chuckle. "Nothing. They're just all lovey-dovey and kissing and stuff, and I don't know. It hurt."

"Okay. You're gonna have to explain that one to me."

"I didn't realize it at first. I was getting mad at her, and assumed it's because everything is so new and she really doesn't know him. But actually, I think it's because of my dad."

He waited for me to continue.

My heart twisted in my chest, and I didn't know how to share. "Because he kissed my mom." That was totally lame. I tried again. "Because he's not here. Because I'm the only one worrying."

Zane didn't say anything. I couldn't even blame him. My words were all over the place. How could things make so much sense in my mind, but come out so jumbled?

Taking a deep breath, I tried again. "Give me a minute. I'll get this out." I paused as my muddled brain found coherent words. "He's only been gone a couple of months, and already things are going back to normal. And I'm not ready for it. I'm worried that without his wisdom and advice, we'll do stupid things."

"Like getting a boyfriend you hardly know?"

"Exactly!" I sighed. "Except my mom thinks it's wonderful that Maralyn has this guy and is encouraging her behavior, and I'm still—I don't know—I'm not liking the way they were kissing. He hasn't even taken her on a date yet, and already, they're making out. And he's giving her flowers and they're snuggling on the couch and . . . and . . . that's what my dad did. For my mom. That was his thing. That's—he always brought home flowers. They were always kissing, and cuddly, and cute. And I don't know. It hurts. A lot. It doesn't make sense. And it hurts."

There. That was as good as it was going to get. Before I knew I'd begun to cry, Zane had started to rock me gently back and forth.

"I'm sorry," he whispered. "It's not fair. And I'm sorry."

"Did you understand any of that?" I wiped at my face again.

"A little." I felt him kiss the top of my head. "I think you're saying that your sister's actions are triggering memories of your father, and your mother seems to think everything is fine. And you're worried that with him gone, there won't be a voice of reason in your lives. Something like that?"

I nodded. "My mom isn't here right now. She's thinks she is. She thinks she has everything under control and that she's moving on, but she's not. And Dad was always the steadier one. He was my rock."

"And now you feel like the only rock in the family is you?"

"Yes." A small tear crept out. "Except I'm the one with autism. How am I supposed to help anyone when I can't even help myself sometimes?"

"Whoa. That's enough." His voice was surprisingly stern. "As your older brother-friend, I'm gonna put my foot down. Stop this negative talk. You already know I think you're a genius, that I think you may be the only sane person I've ever met. You know what I believe you're capable of, so this? This right here? It's done now. No more using this genius ability of yours as a crutch. It isn't a crutch. It isn't something bad—it's amazing! And you have the capability to save the world one day with that mind, but you know what? You won't if you continue to belittle yourself like this. From here on out, you're going to rethink your psyche and focus on your super powers."

I pretended to roll my eyes, but really, I could hardly breathe. "You sound like my dad."

"Good, because someone needs to snap you out of this. You're not stupid, you're not a freak, you're not an idiot, you're not . . . anything you think inside your head or say out loud. You. Are. Amazing."

I couldn't speak. I was in so much of an overdrive, I began to shake. But it was a good shaking, not something scary or bad, but so, so needed. It was like his words were finally sinking in, and I understood that someone actually cared. He was giving me permission not to be what I thought everyone thought of me. I wasn't that girl. I was this . . . this . . . completely different person. I was someone I'd never imagined I could be. Someone my dad always said I was, but no one else ever cared enough to say it. Until now.

FIFTEEN
♥
TICK-TOCK

Zane and I sat there and talked for way longer than I realized. By the time he pulled out his phone to check the time—seven thirty—I blanched. I'd been gone at least two hours! Holy cow, my mom was going to kill me. She had to be worried sick by now.

"I have to go." I jumped up.

"Do you need a ride? I could drop you off." Zane brushed at his shorts as he stood.

I wanted to, but ... "No. I think I'll walk."

"Are you sure? It wouldn't be that big of a deal."

I checked in my pocket for my phone to text my mom before it dawned on me that I didn't have it. Great. I really had to get moving. "Thanks for stopping and making me feel better."

"So cuddle therapy worked, eh?"

I grinned. I had to. "Sure. Whatever."

"You don't sound too convinced. Should we try it again?" He wrapped his arm around my shoulders.

Laughing, I pushed him off. "No."

"Fine, suit yourself. But think how much happier you'd be after another session."

"I have no doubt."

His smile dropped as he looked at me. That gaze connecting with mine—yeesh. It nearly took my breath away.

"Are you sure I can't convince you to take a ride home?"

I shook my head. "And let the world know we were together *again*? I think not."

"Hmm…" One eyebrow rose. "Maybe there's a downside to having such a genius friend."

"Sister."

"Fine. Sister-friend. Happy?"

"Almost."

"What would make you happy?"

You. I took a deep breath. "I'm fine. Anyway, I really should head out."

"So you keep saying.'"

Good grief. "Keep saying? I said it like once. Maybe twice."

"Your point?"

He looked so dang kissable, I could smack him. "Never mind." I chuckled. "Stop being such a dork."

"Nope. You wouldn't love me if I stopped."

Love. There was that word again.

He coughed. "Right, well, um … I don't want to leave. So, are you coming with me in the car, or are we staying here longer?"

I grinned and threw my hands in the air. "You can stay here all you want. I'm walking home." Brushing past him, I headed toward the gap in the chain-link fence.

Zane followed. "Okay. But it'll be crazy to come all the way back here to get the car again."

"Hey, I never said you had to follow me. You're the crazy one."

"I never said I *wasn't* the crazy one. Only pointing out how essentially crazy I am."

I glanced over at him, and my heart skipped a beat. I couldn't believe he was actually walking me home again. Where did this guy come from? And what in the world was I going to do without him?

After a few seconds of silence, my curiosity got the better of me and I asked, "So, how did Loni take the whole 'Ellyn's just a sister' thing?"

His step faltered a bit. "I'd rather not say."

"That bad, huh?"

He sighed. "Yeah. I was an idiot."

"Hey! Who's using negative self-talk now?"

"Touché." He smirked. "But really, I shouldn't have—I mean, I should've seen how talking to you would hurt her."

I felt awful. "I'm so sorry."

"It isn't your fault! I'm definitely the one who keeps pursuing you." He looked back at the bleachers. "Take now, for instance. You told me to go away, and I didn't, did I? I was worried about you, so I sat down and prodded until you finally shared what was wrong."

I bit my lip. "Will Loni be mad about that?"

He shrugged. "I have no idea. She's a girl, so probably. Especially since it was you I was talking to."

My stomach lurched. "This isn't helping."

"I know, sorry. I'm just . . . Why is this so hard, anyway?"

"Because it isn't just about us. It's about other people too. And their feelings matter."

"You were crying. And alone."

"So?"

"*So?*" He looked surprised.

"You came here to stop thinking about me. Not to help me. Isn't that what you said?"

"Yep. Figured running would be a good way to vent some steam and remind myself why Loni matters so much to me." He kicked a rock with his shoe. "Except then I found you and forgot all about Loni again."

"I can't do this." I felt like I was going to be sick.

"Me neither. Why can't life just be simple and uncomplicated?"

I walked faster as my stomach churned. I had to get home. "Let me get this straight. You're upset because you can't have your girlfriend and flirt with me at the same time?"

"I . . . uh . . . well, when you put it that way…"

"You need to make up your mind."

"I have. You won't accept it. I mean, I haven't—yet. But I already know your answer. You told me before."

This time, I understood exactly what he meant. "No."

"See?"

"No. Not even. We barely know each other."

"Ah…" He took a deep breath and slowed his steps. "Which brings us full circle back to your dad."

Wow. I think my mind had just blown. "Yes. It does."

"All right, I'll drop it. You need time, you need space, and I need to figure out what to do on my end. But I'm not giving up! Don't think that I am. There's something here. The timing might not be perfect right now, but it's there. And I don't care what you say, I'm not going to deny it, either."

My heart did somersaults and back flips, and with my lurching stomach, I didn't think I was going to make it. "On second thought, do you think you could run back and get the car?"

He grinned. "Definitely. Had a change of heart?"

"Nope. I think I'm going to be sick."

"That bad?"

I nodded.

He took off. "I'll be back as soon as possible."

"Thanks. I'll meet you in by the ticket counter in front."

I hope.

Five minutes later, my worries about my mom became reality.

"Ellyn Charlotte Dashwood! Where have you been?" she asked as I burst through the door.

I held my stomach and walked past her. It had only gotten worse. "Not now, Mom. I'm not feeling good."

Just then, Zane came through the door.

What was he doing here? "I told you I was fine," I said to him. "You didn't have to come in."

My mom's jaw dropped. "You took off to go on a date with Zane?"

"No."

"And you didn't tell anyone where you were going?"

"No, Mom."

Zane held up his hands. "It wasn't like that, Mrs. Dashwood. We bumped into each other at the school." He gave me a guilty look and mouthed the word "sorry."

I'd told him he should stay outside. Now maybe he understood why.

"What were you doing at the school?" Mom asked me. "You've never left for that long before. I nearly called the cops."

Ugh. None of this was helping. "I have to go." I ran to the bathroom right as a spasm ripped through my stomach. I barely made it to the toilet in time. It was awful. I was positive this wasn't one of those big-brother-friend moments Zane signed up for. I knew he could hear me, even if I'd managed to shut the door first. Why was life so hard? Seriously.

I heard a tentative knock, but couldn't stop the heaves from coming long enough to answer. "Ellyn, are you all right?" Mom asked.

Did I *sound* all right? I could never understand why people asked such odd questions. It was ridiculous. After a few more seconds, I was able to groan out, "No."

I could hear Zane on the other side. "I'm sorry. I found her at the school and we talked for a while, then she said she was going to be sick, so I got her home as fast as I could. I didn't think she'd actually throw up, though."

"Zane, go away!" I coughed and then heaved again. Ugh. "Just go!" I was never going to be able to look at him again. Or my mom. Or anyone else, for that matter.

I didn't hear him leave, but thankfully, the talking stopped, and so did my vomiting. I stood up and washed my face with shaking hands, then brushed my teeth. I was too embarrassed to say goodnight to anyone, so I just headed straight to my room.

My mom came in a few minutes later and walked over to my bed, where I'd curled up under the covers. "Hey, honey. Are you okay?"

"I don't know."

"What's wrong? Did you eat something bad?"

I shook my head. "No. I think it's just stress."

She perched on the edge of the bed and touched my forehead. "And what are you stressed about?"

Honestly? She didn't know?

"How can I help you?"

I attempted to grin. It must've looked more like a grimace because she got worried again. "Are you okay? Do you need to run to the bathroom again? What can I do?"

Ugh. "I'm fine, Mom. I promise. I just need to breathe for a minute and be by myself."

She nodded, but didn't get the hint. "So, about Zane. Did you know he'd be up at the school? What was he doing there so late?"

I. Just. Couldn't. Do. This. Right. Now. "Mo—om," I whined. "Stop."

"What?" She blinked innocently. "Am I not allowed to be curious about what happened?"

"No. Not now, not ever."

She chuckled and tucked my blanket around my shoulders. "Well, guess what, sweetheart? I gave birth to you. I carried you around and fed you and held you—and you're still my baby. You'll always be my baby, and that gives me the right to be curious about you. So deal with it."

Our eyes met. She really was so pretty. I knew that all she wanted was for me to fit in and be happy, and to see me dating someone had to be some sort of amazing dream come true for her. Something she'd been praying about for years. Except—I wasn't dating someone. I wasn't *planning* on dating someone, and every time I thought about that someone I wasn't dating, a tiny piece of my heart began to hurt. And I really couldn't do it. I just couldn't.

"I love you," I said.

She looked shocked—happy, but definitely surprised. "Well, thank you. I love you too. What brought that on?"

I shook my head a little. "Please don't bring up Zane.

Despite what it looks like, we're not a couple. We're not dating."

"He really really likes you."

My jaw dropped. "Mom!"

"What?" She smirked. "He does. I can tell."

"How do you know?"

She shrugged. "Call it mother's intuition. It doesn't matter—he does. And he worries about you and thinks about you and loves being around you." She was getting way too excited.

"Okay, but that still doesn't mean we're together."

"Why would you say that?"

My elbow began to itch, and I needed to hurl again. One part of me just wanted to shout, "Because he has a girlfriend!" But I didn't. I stopped myself just in time. I'd promised them I wouldn't tell anyone, and that included Mom. "Because we're not together, Mom. Trust me. We're just friends."

She stood up and gave a knowing grin. "If you say so."

I winced. "Right. Well, I do. And you'll have to trust me on that."

I felt her light kiss on my forehead and opened my eyes. "When you feel better, I've got leftovers for you in the fridge."

I couldn't even think of eating at the moment. "Okay. Thanks."

"Goodnight. And if things get worse, let me know."

I nodded, but didn't trust myself to speak right then. Another spasm decided to kick me in the gut. Life couldn't get any better if it tried.

{♥}

My upset stomach turned out to be an actual virus. A really awful one. Maralyn headed back to school on Monday, and I was home for two more days after that. Then just as I got better, Katelyn caught it. My mom was positive it would never go away.

People had warned us when we moved that we'd probably pick up all the extra viruses since we weren't immune to them, but wow. New Mexico really knew how to pack a punch! I'd never expected to get that sick.

By the time I made it back to school, Maralyn and Harrison's relationship had jumped notches. I shouldn't have been surprised when I walked into the building Thursday morning and everyone was talking about them, but I was.

They were definitely an item. Sitting together, holding hands, nonstop texting, flirting—the works. Maralyn made sure everyone knew Harrison was her guy and to back off. It was the one subject they couldn't drop—that, and how cute they'd look going to prom together.

I'd forgotten all about prom—but since it was the end of March, the school advertisements were everywhere. They wanted to make sure I never would forget about it again.

My elbow began to itch. Why was there so much pressure to do things you'd never get invited to anyway? Gah. I hated this stuff.

SIXTEEN
♥
SENSATIONAL

Harrison's prom invite for Maralyn was what every girl like my sister dreamed about. Big, loud, public—and incredibly, ridiculously romantic. The type where you wanted to gag, but didn't dare because all the other girls around you were swooning.

He pulled out all the stops, using the school assembly and the principal to execute a perfectly timed invitation by microphone with balloons, flowers, all her friends on the dance team, and also the school mascot uniform. Yes. It was that epic.

But while it was going on, it took me a minute to catch what was happening. The principal invited Maralyn down to the floor. I was sure he was introducing her as one of the new Bloomfield dancers, as the music began and the team started to dance around her. However, once the mascot came out with balloons and flowers, singing one of the latest romantic songs, I knew it was Harrison asking her to prom. He pulled off the mask, and the audience went wild.

In the end, the dancers each held up a letter that spelled, MARALYN WILL YOU GO TO PROM?

Everyone swooned and sighed as she said yes and Harrison scooped her up into a big hug and kiss, and it was enough to make people pass out. I couldn't believe he'd gone to all that trouble. It was incredible, really. And in a way, it made me like him just a tiny bit more. Mostly because he had no problem announcing to the world that she was his. With as flamboyant as she was, she needed that. She needed someone in her life who matched her enthusiasm.

Though I'd completely prepared myself for it, when Zane asked Loni to prom, it hurt a lot more than I expected. His invitation was much more subdued and private, and she made sure to tell me every detail. He'd bought her favorite flowers and taken her for a walk, and then casually asked her if she'd like to go with him. Of course, she gushed and hugged him and said, "Yes!"

"Isn't that the most perfect way to ask a girl to prom?" she asked me as we were heading out of class.

Actually, if I were to be asked, that's the exact way I'd prefer it. "Yes. Totally."

She sighed and clutched her books to her chest, as if she was trying to make this all that much more uncomfortable for me. "I mean, don't get me wrong. Maralyn definitely had the prom invite of the century, but as for me, I completely get why Zane didn't go all out. It just isn't his way."

Did I detect a sort of malice in her voice? "Did you wish he had?"

She plastered on a fake smile and walked a little faster. "Of course not! Why would I? I mean, he's one of the most popular guys at school, and he could totally outdo stupid

Harrison Crawford if he wanted to. It wasn't like he needed to compete. I'm just grateful he finally remembered to ask me at all!" With that, she stomped off, leaving a lot of confused stares following after her in the crowded hall.

One girl stopped me. "Who's taking Loni to prom?"

I just shrugged, put my head down, and headed to my next class. It wasn't my fault she wanted to rant publicly in the hallway, was it? Maybe she and Zane weren't trying to keep everything a secret anymore. Who cared, anyway?

I rounded the corner of the hallway and ran smack-dab into some guy. Papers went flying everywhere. "Sorry!" That's what I got for keeping my head down.

"Hey!" he shouted, clearly angry. "What are you doing?"

Everyone around us started laughing.

I felt like such an idiot. "Sorry. Sorry. Sorry." I dropped my stuff and began to collect his papers. "I was thinking about something and ran right into you."

"Thanks," he grumbled as I handed them to him. Then he looked at me. His face went white. "Oh, Maralyn! I'm so sorry. I didn't know it was you. I didn't mean to get so mad."

I grinned wryly and shook my head. "I'm not Maralyn. She's my twin."

"Oh! You're the girl Zane talks about all the time. Wow. You really do look just like your sister."

"Uh—thanks." Was this one of Zane's friends? "Do you know him?" Okay. Sure that was probably not one of my brightest questions, but I wanted to know *how* he knew him.

"You don't know who I am, do you?"

"Uh, no. Should I?"

He chuckled. "I'm Zed. Yeah, Zane and I go way back. We were even on a baseball team together."

Sometimes I forgot Zane was this all-star athlete. "Oh."

"And he's my older brother."

Whoa! "Brother?"

"He talks about you all the time." He slipped his arm into the strap of his backpack. "The genius."

I blushed. "Not really. I just think differently." I bent over and picked up my things.

He was still waiting for me. "Well, whatever it is, I'm glad he knows you. He's been so much happier ever since he met you. I wasn't sure if he'd ever come back around after my dad did the dating ban." Glancing over slyly, he asked, "So, are you guys going to prom together? Just curious to see if he was brave enough to disobey our dad."

I was pretty sure the drama in this school would never end. "Uh, no. Not at all." I almost added he'd already asked someone else, I stopped myself just in time.

He looked at me curiously. "Huh. I would've thought for sure he'd have gone anyway. So, are you already taken?"

"For . . . for prom?"

"Yeah. Is that why he didn't ask you? Someone else already has?"

I laughed. "No."

"You've got to be kidding me!" He looked shocked. I was just about to take it as a compliment when he blurted out, "Wow! He must like his car more than I thought!"

"What do you mean?"

"Oh, you don't know? Our dad says if he ever catches Zane on a date, he'll sell the car."

I choked. "Really? Isn't that a bit barbaric?" I mean, honestly. What parent does that?

He smirked. "Not when it comes to Dad's oldest. I can

get away with anything, mainly because I'm the youngest. But Zane—yeah, Zane gets the hard treatment. Plus, Dad's ticked Zane doesn't want to run his million-dollar company. I'd do it, but Dad doesn't think I've got the grades or the business savvy to pull it off." He paused at a doorway as the warning bell rang. "Not that I blame my dad. He's put everything he's got into building up this business—it means too much to him not to pass it on Zane."

"So you side with your dad?"

He looked at me for a minute, taking in every detail of my face. I had no idea what he was thinking, but it was slightly uncomfortable. One eyebrow rose. "On second thought, you really don't look much like Maralyn."

I blinked. What was he saying?

"And honestly, I'm not convinced you're as smart as you pretend to be, either. If you were, you'd be a lot more careful who you hung out with and what you did in public."

Was he telling me to back off from his brother? Was this some sort of verbal ambush or something?

"I'd stay far away from Zane, if I were you."

"Nothing like saying it like it is."

He grinned and waggled his eyebrows. "Nope. I prefer to be pretty straight with people. I've been curious about you for a while now. Glad I had the opportunity to see just what my dad is fighting against. It's interesting, really. And for the record, I don't think you're worth it."

"What do you mean?" I hated when I stood there, trying to make sense of what people were saying. Why couldn't I walk away? Obviously, he was trying to hurt me. Why stay and listen to it? Because I'm me. Because I make no sense at all. Ever.

"Clearly, the fact that you're still standing here solidifies my argument. Tell Zane to pick an actual genius next time. I can't handle this level of idiocy." With that, he turned and walked into the classroom.

I had the strongest urge to punch him in the face. And cry, though punching him in the face was seriously outweighing the crying part. A couple of kids looked at me and laughed as they headed into class. I glanced up and realized I was in the freshman wing.

Ugh. How did I follow that loser all the way to his class and get this turned around?

The final bell rang.

Nice. Now I was late, too.

"Maralyn, are you okay?"

I turned to see Skyler heading toward me. "I'm Ellyn."

"Oh, sorry. You guys look so much alike."

I wish. Apparently, not everyone thought so. "No big deal."

"Are you lost?"

"No." Just an idiot.

He looked down the empty hall and then back at me. I probably seemed really weird, standing there, doing nothing. "What class do you have next?"

"I don't know." My mind was racing too much. "I have to go."

He put a hand on my arm. "Whoa. Okay. Let me help you. You don't look that great."

"So I've been told." I pulled my arm away from his grasp. "I'm fine. Just don't touch me for a minute. I need to breathe."

He looked way out of his depth and a bit scared of me.

I just wanted to get far away from this craziness. I began to walk down the hall.

"You're going the wrong way."

I'm not sure how many times he'd said that, but I'm positive it took more than once before I heard. I stopped and turned back around. "Oh." Then I began to head the way I'd come. "Sorry." All at once, I wanted to cry. Lots. As in, more than the amount was allotted to still look pretty. This was the "I'm-so-jealous-of-Loni-and-hate-Zane's-brother" cry. The ugly cry.

"I'm really worried about you." Skyler walked next to me, but was careful not to touch me.

"I'm not okay. But you don't have to be worried. I need to be alone."

"But you're in school. You're technically not supposed to be alone. And especially not out here in the ninth-grade hallway while class is going on."

"I know."

"So are you heading back to your class? I can walk with you."

"It doesn't look like you're giving me much of a choice anyway."

He grinned. "No, it doesn't, does it?"

We walked together in silence to the main hall. "What hour is this?" My brain was seriously not thinking. I was completely fried.

"It's fifth."

"Oh, yeah. Chemistry."

"Great. Let's get you there."

It was the last place I wanted to be, but was probably the best place for me. Even though I was pretty sure I wouldn't be able to concentrate on anything, I definitely didn't want to be crying right now. And if I went home, I'd definitely be crying.

After a little bit, Skyler asked, "So, is Maralyn excited about prom?"

"You can't help yourself, can you?"

"What do you mean?'"

"You always have to bring her up. You've clearly got it worse than I thought."

Skyler looked surprised. "You can tell?"

I wanted to laugh. Had it been any other day, or at any other time, I would have. Instead, I settled for a grin. "Yeah. It's kind of obvious."

He nodded. "I'm crazy, aren't I?"

"For having a thing for my sister, who's in high school?" I shrugged. "Other than the jailbait issue, I'd say you're pretty normal. Everyone usually finds themselves crushing on her sooner or later."

"Everyone? Is it really that bad?"

"I don't know. I wouldn't say it's bad. She's pretty cool."

He looked worried. "Sorry. I didn't mean to insult her. I was just surprised to hear that so many other people like her too."

I finally laughed. "Here's a rule of thumb most guys don't seem to get. Are you ready?"

He looked at me funny.

"Chances are, if you think she's awesome, there's a ton of other guys who are thinking the exact same thing. And, for the record, everyone thinks Maralyn is awesome."

"I'd love some pointers on how to win her over, but I think I'll stick to letting her go for now. I realize that from her perspective, I'm the last person she'd ever notice. Which is fine. But I love the energy and happiness she brings into a room. She's got this bubbly personality that's contagious."

And that right there was the difference between me and my sister. And the reason why I love her to death, but know I'll never be half the happy light source she is. She just glows.

"For the record, I think you'd be good for her."

"Really?" He smiled.

"Yeah, but she'll have to figure that out on her own."

SEVENTEEN
♥
PROM FEVER

"Are you sure this dress looks good on me?" Maralyn asked for the fourth time.

I could feel a headache coming on. "Yes." We'd been to every store in the Farmington Mall and every bridal shop from Durango to Kirtland for two weeks now, and she still hadn't found "the dress."

"Does it really matter?" I groaned as I sat down on a padded chair near the dressing room. "You're only going to wear it for a few hours anyway, and Harrison isn't going to notice it as much as you think he will."

She popped her head out of the nearest stall. "Are you kidding me? He'd better notice this dress, after all the trouble I'm going through to get it!" She shut the door, and I heard rustling as she tried on the next one. There were five dresses in that stall with her. I had no idea how they all fit in that tiny room, but they did. So far, she'd tried on three, the last one being my favorite. Of course, I had a favorite in every store we went to. She just refused to acknowledge that it was her favorite too.

I sighed. "I should've brought my Kindle."

"Come on. You know you love this," came a muffled voice from the stall.

"Yeah, as much as I love homework." I brought both my legs out in front of me. "Actually, I believe this is considered worse than homework."

"How is it that you're female and you hate shopping?"

"I refuse to deem this question worthy of an answer. Just because I'm female does not make me instantly attracted to shopping. Besides, what's the point? It's not like I'm going anywhere anyway."

I heard a few more rustling noises, and then Mara opened the door, wearing a gorgeous frothy purple gown. One of those princessy ones that go to the floor and poof out. "What do you think?"

I was a bit speechless. It wasn't her usual style, but it was so pretty on her.

"Well?" she prompted.

"Yes. I think it's perfect."

"Seriously?" She put a hand on her hip, and the whole dress belled out to the side with her. "You say that with every dress."

"Not true. And this one is just—I love it. It really is my new favorite. You look like Cinderella."

She turned and examined herself in the three-way mirror, lifting the sides of her skirt with her hands and letting it swoosh back and forth. She grinned, and her eyes met mine through the glass. "It's really fun. I feel like a princess in it."

"Once you go princess, you can never go back."

She giggled and then glanced at the price tag. "Ugh. I

would like the one that cost the most."

I began to panic and bit my lip. "How bad is it?"

Mara shook her head. "Bad."

Her idea of bad and mine weren't even in the same wallet. "Anything over fifty dollars is bad to me."

She coughed. "Yeah, well, all the dresses are way over that. This is like, dipping-into-savings-account bad."

"More than two fifty?" I gasped.

Turning from side to side, she examined the dress again and whimpered. "Yeah. More than that."

"No way. Take it off. We'd never be able to face Mom." I couldn't breathe.

"I know…" Her voice trailed away as she examined herself. "But I just want to be in it a few minutes longer."

"You really do look amazing." I got up and walked over to the dangling tag. "Two eighty-five? Yikes." It was soft. Layer after layer of chiffon made it a dancing dream. "Maybe I could convince Mom to combine our dress money so you can get it."

"What?" She looked stunned. "Why would you do that? No. You need one too."

"I'm not going. It's not like I'd use it for anything."

"Why do you say that? I'm sure Zane will ask you any day now. I mean, we still have three weeks."

"No, he won't. Trust me on this."

"Did you guys have a fight or something? What happened? "

My elbow started to itch, and I was still having a hard time breathing. "Stop, please."

Mara glanced over at me. "Okay. I'll stop."

Why did I not believe her? "Thank you."

"Though, you have a funny way of showing guys you like them." *And there she goes again.* "If you really wanted a date,

Jenni James

you should've made it obvious how you felt about the guy. He would've taken you to prom for sure."

I walked away.

"Ellyn! Wait. I still have another dress to try on."

I pushed past racks of clothes and made my way to the front of the store. I needed space. I needed time. I needed to breathe. Once I reached the main section of the mall, I headed over to an empty bench by a planter and sat down. I put my face into my hands so I wouldn't have to see the world around me and rubbed my temples.

I couldn't do this. I couldn't keep Zane's secret *and* deal with my family's lack of understanding. I couldn't handle this unnecessary drama. It was a complete waste of time, and too painful.

And I was freaking out way more than I usually do. I took a deep breath and calmed the rising panic in my chest. It was going to be okay. It really didn't matter to anyone who Zane took to prom. In about three weeks, when he walked into the dance, everyone would know he had a girlfriend anyway. It wasn't a slight on me.

It was just life.

I didn't even know what the big deal was, anyway. Why dress up and go to prom? I couldn't imagine my mom spending a ton of money on me just so I could look "pretty." And then what? I didn't have a date. I didn't have friends to hang out with. I'd be there by myself, watching Maralyn having this amazing time and listening to her friends chatter. How is it fun to go to a dance by yourself when everyone else has a date and you're sitting on the sidelines, watching?

I felt a strange tightening in my chest. Then deep sadness washed over me. I was tired of being in the shadows, the one

144

no one really saw unless it was to exclaim about how odd I was. It hurt. And it wasn't fair.

"There you are!" Maralyn said as she walked up to the bench. "I still had another dress to try on. Why did you leave?"

I sighed and looked up at her. "Because I was done."

It was as if she finally noticed that I hadn't been trying on dresses with her this whole time because she suddenly asked, "Aren't you going to prom?"

"No."

She sat down next to me, and I had to scoot over. "But why not? Everyone wants to go to prom! You need to try on dresses, too. Why haven't you been?"

Why did I have to answer the same questions constantly? "Because I don't want to go."

"Why?"

My hands started to shake, and I felt my chest tighten again. "Because I don't want to go someplace where I'll be bored." There. Maybe now she'd understand.

Mara laughed. "Bored? Are you kidding? With everyone dancing? It'll be way too fun to be boring." She turned toward me. "Are you sure Zane's not taking you?"

Oh, my gosh. "Yes, I'm sure he's not taking me. And yes, I'm sure it'll be really boring."

"Oh! Because you don't have a date." She grinned. "Well, I can help with that."

I was going to lose it. I could feel everything within me boiling. "No. Don't."

"Yes. It'll be so easy. If Zane can't go for whatever reason, I know like ten guys who'll totally take you."

"No."

"Yes! It'll be so fun! You have to come with me." She tugged on my arm. "Come on—let's go choose a dress for you. I feel bad that you haven't tried any on. Once you do and see how gorgeous you look, you'll be all about prom and begging for me to get a date for you."

I pulled my arm away. "No, I won't." My voice raised a few notches. "I won't ever be happy there. I'll never like it. I'll be ignored and miserable and feel completely stupid and out of place. I'm not going. Period."

"Why would you feel stupid?"

"Why?" I stood up. "Because whatever poor guy you set me up with would be around me a total of fifteen minutes before he'd be wishing he was anywhere else. He'd know I'm weird within the first minute of meeting me. And then what?" I threw my hands in the air. "You want me to sit around like some wallflower and watch you and your friends dance? How does that sound fun? It doesn't. Prom just isn't my thing. And that's cool. It doesn't need to be. You can have a great time. I'd rather sit this one out at home, thanks."

She shook her head. "If you don't learn to let go, you'll never learn to live."

I was stunned into silence. I hated it when my sister was right.

EIGHTEEN
♥
PARTY OR BUST

A couple of days later, Skyler approached me in the hall after school. "I'm throwing a party this weekend at my parents' pool. Dress casual, and expect hamburgers, hot dogs, and soda, low key and easy. Would you and your family like to come?"

I wasn't so sure. I'd seen teen pool parties in the movies, and they looked intimidating. "Will there be a lot of people?"

"No. It'll be us and maybe a few of my parents' friends or something to welcome your family to the neighborhood. Totally easygoing."

Maralyn smiled as she walked by, but didn't stop and say anything. Instead, she peered through the open doorway leading outside, close enough to eavesdrop, but not close enough to consider herself part of the conversation.

I watched Skyler glance in Mara's direction a few times, but she didn't look over. He spoke louder. "So, yeah, let your family know and we'll get together. I think it'll be something fun for everyone. You know how cool parties can be."

Mara must've heard the word "party" because she asked, "What are you guys talking about?"

"A pool party my parents are hosting in their backyard. " Maralyn seemed to perk up a bit knowing there was a swimming pool, but not enough to accept the offer. "Oh, sounds fun." She looked away again, as if she was expecting someone.

I waited a few seconds, like I thought she was thinking it over. "Thanks. We'll tell our mom."

Skyler nodded and then walked over and touched Mara's shoulder. "Harrison is invited too."

All at once, Mara's demeanor changed completely. She smiled. "That's really sweet. I'll let him know."

I looked over at Skyler, but I couldn't catch his eye.

His grin matched hers. "Cool. It's this Saturday at four, casual barbecue. I'll give you the address and details tomorrow at school."

"Awesome," Maralyn threw over her shoulder as she stepped outside. "We'll be sure to come."

I decided to follow her. "Thank you for thinking of us."

He seemed happy enough, and not like my sister had nearly dismissed him until he had the insight to invite Harrison.

I really didn't think much about it until Saturday when my family headed to the barbecue—all of us except Maralyn. She'd be riding with Harrison—and he still hadn't shown up by time we left. We'd come wearing swimming suits under our shirts and shorts, flip-flops, and carrying a yummy garden salad my mom had whipped together that morning.

"Welcome! I'm Jeanine." Skyler's mom was a large, boisterous woman, all chuckles and soft rolls in elegant attire. Her jewelry and manicure matched the rest of her to a T. I liked her instantly.

"I'm so glad you've come." She waved her arm, beckoning everyone into the finely decorated home.

"Wow," Katelyn whispered as she crossed the threshold next to me. "Even *we've* never had a house this nice!"

"It is a lovely home," Mom responded loudly to cover up her daughter's faux pas.

"Thank you, dear. Now head on to the back and see the treat we've decided to surprise you with." She bustled them through the house and out double doors that led to a back patio. The smells were wonderful.

"I hope you girls are hungry. Skyler has been cooking up a storm!"

"We're starving!" Katelyn said. "I can't wait to eat. When's dinner?"

Just then, a cell phone went off.

"Oh, that's mine." Mrs. Brandon went to answer it, then bustled back out again. "On second thought, they can leave a message! I've got company." She grinned and turned to my mom. "So, what's your first name, Ms. Dashwood? I've heard so much about you and your girls, I feel like I know you already."

"Please call me Alice," my mom said as they walked outside.

The backyard was completely transformed into a landscaper's dream, a beautiful party haven with a full, gorgeous backyard kitchen. The counters were made of brick and stone, with artfully scattered potted herbs for decoration.

Skyler waved from the barbecue grill. He stood on lush grass right in front of a large created pond with a waterfall and a little bridge. His mom wasn't kidding. He *had* been cooking. There was a large mound of steaks, burgers, and hot dogs near his elbow, much more than any of us could eat during a party.

The backyard went on for quite a ways. "You have some very beautiful landscaping out here," my mom said as she walked over to the countertop and placed her salad next to the several bowls already there.

"Thank you. Make yourself at home. The Benallys—Stephanie and Daniel—will be here soon, and I'm sure you'll love them. They have girls around the same age as your daughters. We thought all the girls would have fun together."

"How nice!" Mom gave me a tight smile—of one of her, "You'd better be polite and enjoy yourself" smiles.

"What are their names?" I asked. There. That sounded like I was interested, right?

"Lauren, Alexis, and Lilly." She waved toward a little walking path. "If we follow these stones around the corner, you'll find the swimming pool. You're more than welcome to dive right in, if you'd like."

Skyler's phone went off loudly. He jumped and reached into his pocket as we all turned around. "It's Aunt Linda," he said. "You'd better answer it."

"Aunt Linda?" Jeanine looked surprised as she walked over to her son's outstretched hand. "Was she the one who tried to call earlier?" She placed the phone against her ear. "What's up? Are you okay?" She gasped. "What? Al? Are you sure it was him? We'll be there right away!"

We waited a few more minutes while Jeanine spoke in hushed tones. Then she passed the phone back over to Skyler. I watched his face turn green as he listened on the other end. His mom looked positively ill too. After he hung up, the two hugged, and then approached us. "Sorry, but we've just received some awful news. We have to leave right now." She wiped at her eyes, flustered. "Sorry. I know we're supposed to have a party, but I can't think right now. We need to hurry."

"Come on, Mom. It's okay." Skyler put his arm around her and turned to leave.

"What?" Katelyn was upset. "Can't you wait until after the party?"

My mom touched her arm to quiet her.

Skyler shook his head. "No. Sorry. We have to leave now. You're welcome to stay and enjoy the meal and pool, if you'd like." He helped his mom up the porch toward the house.

I couldn't believe they'd just leave like that. It was so odd.

"That's fine," Mom said. "We completely understand. I hope everything is okay."

"So do we!" Jeanine looked like she was going to cry. "Where's my purse? Hurry!"

We watched in bewilderment as they took off, bustling through the house.

"Who's Al?" I asked, not fully processing what had just happened.

"I'm going to guess that he's either Jeanine's husband or brother. But with the way Skyler was acting, it was most likely Jeanine's husband—Skyler's dad."

"Oh." I glanced around the empty yard. The barbecue grill was still smoking. "I guess he isn't here—is he?"

Mom must've noticed the grill at the same time I did. She turned it off, then walked over to the patio kitchen and shook her head. There were marinating steaks and burgers sitting out, and all the toppings, sauces, salads . . . "This stuff is going to go bad. Let's clean it up, and then we'll head home."

My chest started tightening. "But we don't know where anything is or where it goes."

Mom's eyebrows rose. "Then we'll figure it out."

"You want me to go through other people's stuff?"

She took a deep breath. "Ellyn, I want you to stop stressing about this, okay? We're going to do a service project now. This family needs our help. Something tragic just happened, and we will not leave the place looking like it does. So I need you to go into the house, rummage through their kitchen and pantry—I'm sure there's a pantry. Find it—and bring back any Ziploc bags and plastic wrap or foil you can find. We're going to put this all away."

She looked over at my little sister. "Katelyn, your job is to collect all the clean silverware and paper plates and napkins. Let's get them put back in their packaging and find out where they need to go. Okay?"

I glanced around the yard. There was so much here, so much they had done to make the place look festive, and now they couldn't enjoy it. My heart grew a little. Mom was right—this was a service project. The good karma that would come from helping them far outweighed my need not to go through their things. "Okay." I smiled. "I'll see what I can find."

As I headed into the house, I saw a family walking in. "Hello," they called out. "Jeanine? Al? Are you out back?" There was a beautiful light-haired woman, a handsome Native American man, three girls, and a cute guy. I didn't recognize any of the girls. They looked a bit older than me. They must be the Benallys.

"Hi," I answered a tad awkwardly. "They had to leave just now. The party is canceled."

"What?" The mom looked worried. "Is everything okay?

Are you sure they canceled the party? That doesn't seem like them." She pulled out her phone and began to text.

"Yes. We're just cleaning up so the food doesn't go bad, and then we'll be leaving."

Two of the girls were totally appraising my clothes—they didn't seem to be the nicest of people. But the other one— she had darker coloring and beautiful, thick black hair—was smiling. I really didn't want to be answering their questions. "Would you like to head out back and meet my mom? She probably knows more than I do. And she'd love to say hello."

"Yes, thanks." The family brushed past me and headed straight for the patio doors. They'd obviously been here many times and knew the Brandon' house well.

I began my search in the large gourmet kitchen. There were several drawers, so I started with the closest one.

"That's for the silverware." I jumped a bit at the voice behind me. It was the pretty dark-haired girl. We were the only ones in the kitchen. "Which drawer are you looking for? I could probably help you."

"I . . . uh . . . I'm trying to find something to cover the food with. And Ziploc stuff. You know, those things." Great. I was totally sounding like a dork.

She giggled, but not mockingly—more friendly. "Yeah, this place is tough for finding stuff. Hang on. I think they're in here." She turned around and walked over to a pantry door. Mounted on the inside of the door was a large bracket of shelves that held all of the foil, plastic, and Ziploc boxes anyone could ask for.

"Wow. That's a lot."

She grinned and pulled out a few boxes, and then walked back over. "The Brandons love to cook, so they always have everything on hand."

"Thank you. You guys must be really close friends. You've obviously been here a lot."

"They're some of my parents' favorite people in the world. They're really sweet. Have you met Skyler yet?"

"Yes! He's awesome."

She nodded. "He's definitely a wonderful guy. They all are. Just a great family."

"Who's wonderful? Are you replacing me already?" The cute guy who'd come with the Bennallys walked back into the kitchen.

"This is Sean Benally," the girl said. "Don't ever fall for his drama." She rolled her eyes. "I'm Lilly Price."

"Hi." Her smile was so contagious. "I'm Ellyn Dashwood. One of the Dashwood twins."

"Ah." Sean laughed as he wrapped an arm around Lilly's waist. "I've heard about you two."

"You have?"

"Yep. Seems like more than one girl is jealous that you've captured the heart of Harrison Crawford."

Lilly visibly shuddered. "Ugh. Don't mention his name in my presence."

Now here was a girl with information. "Why?" I asked.

She shook her head. "Sorry. Are you the one dating him?"

"No, but something seems off with the guy. I mean, he's nice enough, but I'm worried about my sister."

She and Sean glanced at each other. He shook his head a bit as if to tell her not to say anything.

"What?" I asked. "What have you heard?"

Lilly growled. "What have I heard? Ha! More like, what have I experienced?"

"Experienced? How long have you known him?"

"Too long! He and his sister moved here at the beginning of their senior year last year."

"Wait. As in, this past September?"

"No, the one before that."

"But he's a senior now." I looked from one to the other. "I'm confused."

Lilly's jaw dropped.

Sean chuckled. "That's something I didn't know."

"How many classes is he making up?" Lilly tossed her hair over her shoulder and leaned on the kitchen counter.

I shrugged. "No clue. I assumed this was his first time as a senior—so, wait. Why wouldn't he just do night school and GED out? Why go back to high school at all? How embarrassing."

One dark eyebrow rose to match Lilly's wry grin. "Honestly, ten bucks says he came back to chase new meat."

"New meat?" What? "Oh! You mean the girls."

"Yep." Sean coughed.

"Right." It was all beginning to make sense. "So he's clearly stuck in an immature reality."

"And he's older than he appears to be." Sean was beginning to look concerned. "So, what does he do on his dates with your sister?"

"Wouldn't you like to know?" Harrison said as he and Maralyn walked into the room.

NINETEEN
♥
BREAK IT UP

Maralyn looked mad. With her hand on her hip and her mouth in a straight line, she was barely holding in her rage. "Do you always talk about people when they're not around?" Her eyes clashed with mine.

"Sometimes," I admitted truthfully. My elbow began to itch.

She glanced over at Sean and Lilly, but reserved the brunt of her anger for me. "Well, it's rude." Folding her arms, she continued, "And for the record, I already knew Harrison was repeating his senior year. So if there's anything else you'd like to add, let's go ahead and throw it on the table now."

Harrison placed an arm around her shoulder. "Shh… it's okay. We really should be flattered that they took time out of their lives to discuss ours. It's the only way to look at it."

Sean and Lilly fidgeted next to me.

I rolled my eyes and pushed away from the counter. "Heaven forbid we care about you." Shaking my head, I collected the Ziplocs and plastic wrap and walked outside. I was done. There was no way Mara was going to get me into an argument at someone else's house. Besides, Mom would kill us both. I had to leave.

"Just walk away!" Maralyn hollered behind me.

I almost turned back around, but didn't. However, I did hear Lilly say, "It wasn't Ellyn's fault. Let's just say that some of us know Harrison much better than you do, and we'll be worried about any heart he has wrapped around his finger *this* week…"

"That's enough, Lilly." Harrison's deep voice was louder than hers.

"This week?" Mara sounded mad. "What do you mean by that?"

I was having a hard time breathing. It sounded like there was some bad blood between Harrison and Lilly, and she wasn't afraid to call him on it. Too many questions, without enough answers. Why didn't Maralyn see the truth?

"There you are, Ellyn." Mom waved me over as she folded a blue-checkered tablecloth. "What took you so long?"

I blinked and took a deep breath. *Right. We're helping Skyler's family clean up.* "Sorry. Maralyn showed up, and I was talking to Sean and Lilly."

"Lilly! Sean!" Mr. Benally was cleaning up the grill. "Come out and help us put everything away."

Mom set the tablecloth down as Mrs. Benally approached with another one. "Well, it's about time Mara and Harrison showed up. What took them so long?" Mom got the tablecloth from the other woman. "Thank you." Then she turned back to me. "Where are they now?"

"In the kitchen."

She sighed and cupped her mouth as Sean and Lilly opened the back door. "Maralyn, come out here and help too!"

I felt a rush of panic. The last thing I wanted to do was get caught standing next to Mom when my sister walked out. "Where do you want me to begin with the food?" I asked quickly.

Mrs. Benally whisked the last cloth off the nearby table and answered for my mom. "Why don't you have Lilly and Sean help you too? The girls are already collecting the unused dishes, so if you can start putting away the food on the porch, that'd be great." She then seemed to remember my mom. "Er, is that all right?"

Mom glanced at me and said, "Of course."

"What do you need?" Maralyn asked from the doorway. Harrison came up behind her.

I went to the patio and didn't make eye contact with Mara. Instead, I began to rip off sheets of plastic wrap and covered the different salads and condiments. I didn't know if Lilly and Sean heard Mrs. Benally, but they had no problem picking up Ziploc bags and going to work.

Within a few minutes, we'd prepared most of the food to go back in the house. I was putting the lid back on some barbecue sauce when I overheard my mom talking to Maralyn.

"So, why were you guys so late getting here?"

"I don't know. Harrison was late picking me up—he said something happened to slow him down."

They both looked over at Harrison, who was collecting the lawn chairs and bringing them back to the porch.

"Did he tell you what happened?" Mom asked her.

"Not really, but he looked kind of freaked out when he got to the house."

"Well, that's everything." Lilly washed her hands and turned off the faucet. "Are we ready to take it inside?"

Dang it. So much for eavesdropping.

Sean stacked as many bowls of food as he could before making his way to the door. "What's taking you two so long?"

I chuckled and started piling my arms full of condiments as Lilly grabbed bags of marinating meat.

"Hold the door open for us," she said to Sean.

"Sure. Now I've gotta do everything?"

"Good grief." She chuckled as she brushed past him. "Carrying a few dishes and being a gentleman—you're already doing everything."

He gasped. "Are you mocking me?"

"You'd better believe it."

He winked as I walked past and then he said, "Thanks. Don't mind me and Lilly. We've been arguing for years."

"*Years*." She opened the fridge and set a bunch of things inside, then cleared space for Sean's dishes.

"See?" Sean grinned and started to hand over the bowls. "It's how I know she still loves me."

"You're going to get it one day," Lilly grumbled as she placed another one on a shelf.

He laughed. "Empty threats, empty threats."

I let the two banter, just enjoying their playfulness. It was something my mom and dad used to do, these little one-up word games. Dad used to say he married Mom because she was the only one who could keep up with him. Mom used to say she was the only girl who wasn't afraid of him, and it was a dang good thing they got married since she was pretty sure no one else would've put up with him.

It's the relationships like Sean and Lilly's, like my mom and dad's that I relate to most. They're not out to hurt one another, and the joy—the sparkle that lights up their eyes as they tease—is perfection. To me, it's normal.

Which was probably why I worried so much about Harrison and Maralyn. There wasn't playfulness—just intensity, and feelings, and . . . I don't know . . . they were too serious about everything. It wasn't right, was it? Something seemed off. And the more I pieced together about Harrison, the more I wondered how right I'd been all along.

{♥}

A couple of days later, my worry about Harrison became reality when Maralyn burst through the bedroom door and jumped on the bed above me. I'd been doing homework with my iPod on, but quickly turned it off once I heard her sobbing.

"What's wrong?" I asked as I climbed out of bed and peeked at her.

"Everything!" she wailed before turning her back to me. Her shoulders shook hard. I reached out and touched her.

"Hey, it's okay. Do you want to talk about it?" I really had no idea how to handle situations like this. You'd think I'd be used to them, but I really wasn't. All I knew was that I needed space and time alone, but Maralyn did better talking and venting it out.

She continued to cry. This really was something extremely devastating for her.

I tried again. "Come on—just tell me about it. You'll feel better."

"No, I won't! You're going to harp on about Harrison and how you were right, and I don't want to hear it."

My stomach dropped. All at once, I had a strong urge to punch the guy in the face. "What did he do? Did he touch you? Hurt you? What?" I pushed her shoulder. "Tell me!"

Mara slowly turned around. Her face was in complete shock. "Wow. I don't think I've ever seen you mad before."

Was I mad? I could feel rage coursing through me. "I guess I am. But really, he'd better not have tried anything. I'll destroy him."

"I can see that." She wiped at her eyes as she propped herself up on her elbows. "No, it isn't anything like that. He didn't hurt me physically. Just my heart. I think it's literally breaking."

I really was going to kill him. "Tell me what happened."

She blinked, and then her shoulders began to shake again. Suddenly, she was crying, and my rage toward Harrison tripled.

It took every ounce of control not to shout at her. But really, I could feel my whole body overreacting in a way I wasn't comfortable with, but it created this new sense of power or something. All over me. "Tell me."

"He's moving! To Farmington. Okay? He's not going to prom, or school, or anything. His parents have kicked him out of the house, and he has to go live with someone else in Farmington. A friend, or aunt, or something—I don't know. He hasn't told me yet. All I know is that he's leaving me and he can't see me anymore and I'm going to . . . I'm just going to die without him!"

"Wait. Are you serious?" I couldn't even process everything she was saying.

"Yes! It's awful!"

He was actually getting kicked out of his house? "Um, so, why? What did he do?"

"I don't know. He wouldn't tell me. He said it was bad, though, and his parents found out and they're super mad and nothing is making sense. Nothing."

"Um…" I didn't know what to say. I let her cry. I felt bad for her, but at the same time, I was relieved, too. If he screwed up so much that his parents kicked him out, he was not a good guy. Thank goodness he and Maralyn were being separated now and not later after he did something to hurt her too.

I quietly left the room and walked into the kitchen. My mom was wiping at her eyes. "Did you hear about Harrison?"

I nodded. "Yeah."

"It's awful. I feel so bad for her. I was really hoping he'd be the guy to break her out of this funk she's been in." Maralyn had been acting weird lately? I hadn't noticed.

Mom opened the dishwasher and looked inside, then shut it. "I don't feel like doing anything right now." She plopped down on a chair, so I sat down next to her.

"What do you think he did?" I was hoping to get any information I could.

"I don't know. I don't even care. I just care about Maralyn's heart breaking so badly right now."

My jaw dropped. "You don't even care what he did to get himself kicked out?" Was I hearing her correctly?

She looked at me and then straightened up a bit. "Of course I care—I wasn't saying that. I just meant that I'm more worried about Mara right now than what happened. Her heart is breaking, Ellyn. Breaking. This isn't good."

Since when was Mom so caught up in drama like this that she forgot common sense? "Well, yes, I'm sure she's sad." I tried to keep my voice as neutral as possible.

"Sad?" Mom let out a sob. "She loves him! And he's been banned from seeing her and she's upset. Do you know what it's like to lose someone you love so much? Do you? It hurts! She literally feels like she's dying because her heart is broken…"

Wow. I looked at my mom for a few minutes while she continued to vent. It wasn't Maralyn she was talking about. I was beginning to understand—it was her. She was missing Dad. He'd left her suddenly, and now this. It was the first time I'd seen her grief. She needed to feel it and accept it. I knew she did, but at the same time, it was really hard to see my mom sort of lose it in front of me.

"I'm sorry," I whispered.

Mom looked at me and started to cry all over again. She needed time alone. She needed to process.

After a little bit, I slowly stood up and walked away. I found Katelyn in the living room watching a movie. I looked at the time—it was crazy late. "Hey, aren't you supposed to be getting ready for bed?"

She shrugged. "No one told me to."

I doubted if anyone was in a state to tell her tonight. "Well, I am."

Looking up, she made a funny face and asked, "Why is everyone so sad?" The hustler was clearly trying to get out of going to bed.

I didn't know how much I should tell her, so I hedged. "What do you mean?"

Katelyn rolled her eyes and turned off the TV. "You can tell me what's really happening. It's not like I'm blind or something."

Sighing, I sat down on the couch next to her. "Well, Mara is sad because she can't see Harrison anymore, and Mom is sad because she's missing Dad."

"Oh." Katelyn curled up next to me. "I miss Dad too."

"So do I."

She plucked at the button on my shirt. "What can we do about it? Is there something that makes missing Dad better? So we don't hurt as much?"

"Nope." I shook my head. "Only time. Supposedly, it gets better the longer you wait."

"I was afraid of that." She snuggled in closer and then asked, "What do you miss the most about him?"

I don't know. I thought about it for a minute and then answered, "I think I miss all the hours of talking to him. Being able to ask him questions and hear his advice."

"I miss him playing with me. Taking me to the store and then secretly buying me an ice cream cone on the way home. I miss that—having a partner in crime."

Wait until Mom heard that. I chuckled. "A partner in crime, huh?"

She grinned. "He was the best at it."

"Yes. He most definitely was."

TWENTY
♥
THE GUILT FACTOR

"What do you mean, you want me to go to prom with you?"
Out of everything I'd ever heard Maralyn say, this had to be
the absolute craziest.

"Please?" she whined in front of the door of our bedroom,
holding me hostage inside with her. "I don't want to go all
alone. I've already got the dress—I've been planning on
going for forever now. Just be my date. We'll have a blast, I
promise. Then you can see what prom's really like."

It was a week before the big day. Harrison had yet to
answer one text, Facebook post, or email from Maralyn the
whole time. She was an absolute mess. In fact, this was the
first bit of spark I'd seen in her since he'd left.

"Come on—just come." She attempted a smile. "Think
of how much fun it'll be to dress up together."

I was already dreading it. But more than that, I was dreading
her staying here alone during the prom. If I thought she'd been a
wreck before, that would be ten times worse. I was positive of it.

But I really, really didn't want to go. I didn't. I hated the idea of prom. Hated it. And I so didn't want to see Zane there, dancing with Loni. Maralyn was staring right at me, her eyes pleading with mine. "Aren't you mad at me?" I blurted, hoping she'd say yes.

"For what?" She looked at me like I was crazy.

I threw my hands in the air and walked around the room. "I don't know—for talking bad about Harrison to Sean and Lilly the other day. Haven't you wanted to chew me out since then?"

"Uh—sure. I guess. But what does this have to do with going to prom?"

"Because we're fighting?" I answered lamely.

She groaned. "We're sisters. We're supposed to fight. It's part of the family code or something."

"Oh. So, you're not mad?"

"Not mad enough to miss prom." She laughed.

I had to grin. "You're incorrigible."

"What?" She blinked innocently at me. "Haven't you forgiven me over and over again?"

"More times than you know."

"Exactly! See? We're just making up." Grabbing my purse, she headed toward the door. "Now hurry up. Let's get to the mall so we can get you a dress!"

"Ugh. No."

"Too late." She dangled the keys in front of me. "I already asked Mom for the car. She gave me the debit card, and she says there should be enough left over for Chinese food, too."

"I'm sure this could be considered kidnapping," I muttered as I slipped on my flats.

"Not if you go willingly." Mara walked out the door. "Chinese food … It's your favorite."

I wanted to cry. I didn't. But I sure wanted to.

After what seemed like hours of trying on dresses—this time it was *me* being tortured—I finally settled on a beautiful green gown. The long skirt was made of a couple of layers of fun silk. They were lightweight and just seemed to flow and bounce as I walked. With its three-quarter sleeves and sweetheart neckline, I looked like I'd stepped straight off the set of a 1940's movie. It was something I hadn't expected to find, and since we'd waited so close to prom to get it, it was 25% off, too.

I'd thought I'd protest a lot more than I did, but I think I secretly really wanted to wear it. Even if Zane wouldn't be dancing with me, at least he'd see me looking amazing.

Once we'd paid for the dress, I noticed that Maralyn was hanging back a bit in the mall. She seemed to be looking into every store. I hoped she didn't have even more shopping in mind.

"What are you doing?" I asked.

She looked over at me guiltily. "Nothing."

Grinning, I shook my head. "Right. Are you gonna tell me?"

She shrugged and let out a sigh. "I don't know. I was hoping that since we're in Farmington and all, we might run into Harrison."

It was all making sense now. I switched the dress bag to my other hand. "Oh, so *that's* why you were so desperate to get me to prom. You wanted to make a trip to Farmington to find your boyfriend."

"What? No! Not at all. I mean, okay. Yes. Maybe a little bit. But that's *not* why I came up with the idea to go to prom with you."

She looked sincere. I decided to drop it. "So, are we going to eat yet? I'm starving."

She glanced around the mall and then sighed again. "Yeah, why not? The odds of running into him are pretty slim anyway. He's probably not even in town."

"Probably."

"Well, you don't have to agree so quickly. What if he *is* here?"

Oh, my gosh. This was going to be a long day. I could tell. "Chinese? You said something about Chinese?"

Mara grinned and headed toward the mall entrance. "You're right. Let's go eat."

The restaurant was a hubbub of activity—an all-you-can-eat buffet with sushi and Mongolian barbecue. The place was packed, and smelled awesome. We were seated quickly, and then took off toward the buffet. It wound through two rooms, full of entrées.

Mara had her eye on the Mongolian, while I headed straight for the good stuff—sesame chicken. Just as I went for the serving spoon, another hand beat me to it.

"I'm sorry," a deep voice said above me.

I glanced up into the shocked face of Harrison Crawford.

"Ellyn," he whispered, "what are you doing here?"

"Hi," was all I got out.

"Here. You first." He handed me the spoon as he glanced around the restaurant. "Are you alone?"

"No. Maralyn's here too." I looked toward the Mongolian line, but there were so many people, I couldn't see her.

He looked nervous. "She is? Where are you guys sitting?"

"In the other room."

A small glimmer of relief seemed to creep its way across his face.

"Excuse me," a customer said as he brushed past us. We were totally holding up the line.

"Sorry," I murmured, then quickly added a scoop of chicken onto my plate. I didn't know what to do or say.

Thankfully, Harrison seemed a bit more with it. "Well, I'm gonna head back to my table now. It was nice seeing you. Tell Maralyn I said hi." He took off. Just like that—scurried around the long buffet and toward his seat.

I stood there, staring at him with the silly spoon in my hand, as he sat down across from a gorgeous girl.

My heart froze. With the way she was leaning into him and smiling, they were clearly on a date. How in the world was I ever going to tell Maralyn?

"Harrison!" Maralyn's shrill, excited voice silenced the room. I saw her winding her way toward him. "You're here!" She was ecstatic. Her arms went out as if she were about to hug him, but he never stood up. He didn't budge from the table at all. "What's wrong?" she asked as she reached him.

Someone had to get her away from them. I turned around and shoved the spoon back into the orange chicken. Leaving my plate on the buffet, I walked over to her.

"Why haven't I heard from you?" She pointed to his phone. "Why haven't you texted me? Or replied on Facebook? I've been worried sick about you."

He looked like he was about to throw up. "I—I don't know what you're talking about."

"Harrison?"

I put an arm around her shoulders. "Let's go."

It was then that Maralyn seemed to notice the girl, who was staring rather openly and rudely at us both. "Who's this?" Maralyn asked.

He cleared his throat. "This is Sydney."

The girl flipped her hair. "I'm his girlfriend. Who are you?"

Mara choked and stepped back a few paces. "His girlfriend? What are you talking about? Harrison? You already have a new girlfriend?!"

I needed to get my sister out of there right now. I tugged on her shoulder again.

"New?" The girl smirked. "We've been going out for months now."

"What?" I thought Mara was going to punch something. She turned toward Harrison and nodded slowly. "Nice."

He fidgeted in his seat. I think he was worried she'd deck him too.

But surprisingly, she didn't. Mara simply turned on her heel, then walked out of the restaurant and out to the car. I followed, and told the lady behind the register to give me a second and I'd be back with the money to pay for our meals. Mara had my mom's card. But she waved me away. "You're fine. Neither of you ate anything anyway."

"Thanks."

By the time I'd made it to the car, Maralyn was bawling.

"You were right," she said. "You were right. You were right. You were right!"

I didn't want to be right. Not then, not ever. "I'm so sorry," I whispered.

"Why?" She sniffed as she started the car. "You were worried about him. You didn't trust him. You tried to warn me, multiple times, but I wouldn't listen. I should've known better. I should've listened." Her fist hit the steering wheel, hard. "I hate him. I really, really do."

I refused to say anything. I let her stay in the parking lot. It took about fifteen minutes for her to freak out and vent and get everything off her chest. It was better here without the car moving than out on the road.

I'd figured Harrison wasn't the greatest guy out there, and he was definitely hiding something, but I didn't think he was this big of a loser. My sister deserved someone so much better!

{♥}

Unfortunately, the Harrison drama didn't end there. Monday, we got another blow. At the end of school, Skyler caught up with me in the hall.

"Hey, Ellyn. Can I talk to you for a minute?"

"Sure." I shifted my bags and followed him to the music room. "What do you need?"

He ran his hand through his hair. "I don't know if I should be asking this, but my curiosity has gotten the better of me. Is everything okay with Maralyn? She looked a little down today. Do you know what's going on?"

Was it all right to talk to him about her? It was probably fine. I wasn't sworn to secrecy or anything. "I—" I had no idea how to bring this up, so I did what worked best for me and blurted it out. "Harrison had to move to Farmington."

"Yeah, I heard. So is she all right? Is that what's wrong? She's still missing him?"

"Not exactly. We ran into him this past Saturday. He was on a date with his longtime girlfriend, Sydney."

His jaw dropped. "Are you kidding me?"

"Nope."

He shook his head. "That jerk deserves everything he's going to get. Everything." He looked down the hall and then back at me. "At first, I felt kind of bad about his arrest and all that, but now I'm glad it happened. Karma has a way of coming back and kicking someone in the butt when they need it most."

Only one part of that comment stuck out to me, and that was, "his arrest." "What do you mean? What was he arrested for?"

Skyler's eyes went as hard as steel. "If he's lucky, it won't be for murder. But since my dad's still in the hospital, we'll have to see."

TWENTY-ONE
♥
WAIT. WHAT?

My chest tightened. It felt as though my heart had frozen inside it. "What do you mean? Why is your dad in the hospital?" Then I gasped. "The day of the party when something happened to your dad and Harrison came late— is that what you mean?"

"Yes." Skyler clenched his teeth.

"I had no idea your dad was in the hospital. Maralyn said you weren't at school the last week or so. . . Sorry. I've been so caught up in my own life, I can't believe I didn't remember about your dad. What did Harrison do? What happened?" My mind was officially blown. I knew I was chattering, but really? Harrison got arrested? And now this? Where was I when all this was going on?

"Harrison told the cops that he was running late and trying to text Maralyn that he'd be there soon. My dad was walking to his parked truck, which was on the side of the road. He'd just picked up some firewood for our backyard fire pit to make s'mores for our party that night.

"Harrison was distracted by texting and veered to the left, hit the curb in the other lane, freaked out, overcorrected, and missed my dad's truck by mere centimeters. However, when my dad jumped back, Harrison clipped him with the side of his car, and then ran him over with his back tires."

I gasped. "No."

"My dad has been in a coma ever since."

"I'm so, so sorry. I had no idea!"

He looked around the room and then shut the door. "The worst part was that Harrison was so worried about getting caught texting while driving that he took off. He saw my dad lying there on the street, and he drove away."

I slowly shook my head while that sank in. "I can't believe it."

"Thank goodness there were enough witnesses to describe Harrison's vehicle that the cops were able to find him easily enough. There were still pieces of my dad's shirt stuck in his front bumper. He was arrested the next day."

I walked over to a chair and sat down. I didn't think my legs would work much longer. "I'm so sick right now."

He pulled up a chair and sat across from me. "I know. Me too."

Suddenly, I thought of Harrison on his date, and I wanted to fling the idiot through a window. "Why isn't he in jail right now?"

"His parents weren't going to post bail. They thought he should rot in there until his trial to teach him a lesson. I guess he got his girlfriend in Farmington to bail him out. He claimed Sydney was just a friend, but now we know otherwise. His parents kicked him out of the house the next day. He's been living with that girl ever since."

I couldn't even. I just couldn't. It was all was too much to process.

But it was as if I'd released a dam of information from Skyler. He couldn't stop talking.

"I've heard his court date is set for next month. I don't know who he'll get for a lawyer, but it'd better be a good one. Harrison has a lot to answer for. If he'd just stopped and tried to help my dad, this all would've all been so much better. But since he took off—yeah, no. He's going down."

My mind was whirling. It felt as if I were in the middle of a movie or something. "Sounds like he'll get exactly what he deserves." This kind of stuff didn't happen to us. This was the sort of thing that happened to teens in California or New York or Chicago. Not here. Not in little Bloomfield, New Mexico. And it certainly didn't involve people I knew.

It was horrific to imagine.

"Hey." Skyler got up from his chair and knelt in front of me. "Are you okay?"

I let out this weird snort/chuckle thing. "Am I okay? Your dad is in a coma because of some selfish jerk, and you're asking if *I'm* okay?"

He gave a wry grin. "Well, I've had a few more days to mull this over. You seem to be in shock."

"Yep. Probably what this is—a bit of shock."

He took my hands in his and searched my eyes. "It's going to be okay. I mean—it won't. Nothing will be the same again, really. But it'll all work out."

"Does Maralyn know?"

"No, I guess not. I don't know how to tell her, either."

I squeezed his hand. "I'll find a way to do it tonight. Then you can talk to her if you'd like, answer any questions—I don't know. I just—I'm sorry." I stood up. "I need to go. I've gotta get out of here and think." My elbow was beginning to itch again, and all at once, the room seemed to be closing in on me. I had to say something polite, didn't I? Except that I didn't know what else to say. "Um—thanks for sharing." I found my bags. Apparently, I'd dropped them once I'd sat down. I hadn't even noticed. I picked them up and looked at Skyler. "Bye." Then I headed out of the classroom and down the hall as fast as I could.

"Ellyn! Wait up!" Maralyn was running toward me. "Where have you been?"

I glanced back at Skyler's room and then toward my sister. I didn't know which was worse at the moment. "I was . . . I was . . ." My mouth really wasn't functioning at the moment.

"She was talking to me," Skyler said as he walked out into the hall.

"Oh." Maralyn looked between the two of us. "What's going on? Has something happened?"

"Yeah. I have to go. I'll tell you later." I was going to have a full-blown panic attack. I could feel it forming already.

"Wait." She tried to stop me from walking past.

"Actually, I can tell you what's going on, if you're willing to hear it from me," Skyler stepped in.

My eyes connected with Maralyn's. "Do it. Talk to Skyler. It's not going to be easy, but you need to hear what he has to say."

"Is it about Harrison?"

How did she do that? Seriously.

"Yes," Skyler and I said at the same time.

She took a deep breath and then glanced over at him. "Okay. Can we go somewhere private?"

He stepped back and opened the door to his room even farther.

"I'll see you at home." I had to get out of there right now. As in, right this second.

"Okay." Maralyn walked into the classroom, and I bolted, heading for the first outdoor exit I could find. As quick as I could, I made my way home and collapsed on my bed.

I must've fallen asleep because the next thing I remember was Maralyn bursting into our room. "This is all my fault!" She threw her bag on the chair and began to pace the floor. "If Harrison hadn't been coming to pick me up, he never would've texted me to say he was running late. Then he never would've hit Skyler's dad! And now he's going to prison. I know it. All because of me!"

"Whoa. Okay, I don't always understand a ton of what's going on, but this much I do know—you are not now, or ever, to blame for Harrison's stupidity! Ever. Do you hear me?"

"But if it wasn't for that, he'd still be here!" she wailed and plopped down on the floor. "I hate myself so much right now."

"He'd still be here pretending to be your boyfriend while two-timing on you. How is that cool? Are you crazy?"

"I love him! We were so perfect for each other. I don't care if he had another girlfriend. Clearly, he wasn't happy with her because he reached out to me. We were inseparable. Remember? There's a reason for that. I'd found my soulmate! He'd even hinted around that eventually, we'd get married and have kids. You don't just drop those feelings the second you find out the guy—"

"Is a jerk?" I interrupted. "Actually, yes, you do. You drop those feelings and smack yourself across the head and wonder where your brains went. Yes, you let him go."

She looked so lost, staring up at me. "I can't let him go. I can't. I'm just blaming myself. It's so hard to imagine him anything less than perfect."

Maralyn was serious. I couldn't believe it. Her face was so stricken, she actually believed she'd caused Harrison's accident. I was stunned. Slowly, I knelt down on the floor next to her and whispered, "Do you know why people change so quickly when they find out they've been betrayed? It's because they realize their own worth is greater than that person's lies."

Her dark brown eyes were so full of hurt right now. "Skyler's dad could die," she said quietly.

"I know."

"Harrison could've killed someone while texting me."

I took a deep breath. "Maralyn, stop it."

"It's true, though—isn't it? You can't take that back. It's fact."

How dare Harrison share that part of the story—how dare he insinuate that he had a good reason to be texting someone? He must have known Mara would feel guilty. I really wanted to hurt that guy.

"If Skyler's dad dies, I'll die. As in, really die. I will. I couldn't live with it."

What was she saying? "Don't you dare think that way!"

She pushed away from me. "I can't help it. That's how I feel. I know how awful it is to lose a parent! I know! And to have Skyler's dad gone because of me—I wouldn't be able to handle the pressure. I'd die. I know it, I just would."

I reached over and shook her. I didn't know what else

to do. "Maralyn, stop it. Don't say stuff like that. Why would two wrongs make a right? It wouldn't! I need you. I've already lost Dad—I can't lose you. Mom couldn't lose you—or Katelyn! Snap out of it. You need counseling or something. You need help—but not death. I couldn't—stop. Just stop."

She seemed to focus a bit more, as if she'd been gone and now come back to the room all of a sudden. "Breathe, Ellie. Breathe. It's okay. You don't need to panic. I'm here. It's okay."

I was crying. This drama was way too much for me. I couldn't handle anything right now. Why was life so messed up? Was there never going to be any peace? When would the good shine through the bad? I couldn't take it.

There was a knock on the door. It was Mom. "Hey, Maralyn. Skyler's here to see you. Would you like to come out and talk for a minute?"

We looked at each other as I wiped my eyes.

"You need time, don't you?"

"So do you," I reminded her.

She shook her head. "Maybe I do just need to talk to someone."

"He's a really nice guy."

Closing her eyes, she asked, "Is he?"

"Yes."

"And he won't hurt me, or lie to me?"

"I sincerely doubt it."

"Because I'd rather invest my time on something I know is real."

"You don't have to become his girlfriend, you know."

"Ew. I wasn't planning on that!" She made a face.

"You're such a brat. He likes you so much more than you deserve."

She attempted a grin. "Probably." Then she sighed. "Honestly, I need a friend. Someone who can talk me down from this insanity. Someone who can help me make sense of this all."

I nodded. She totally did. "Then he's the perfect guy for the job. He'll genuinely listen."

"Hang on, Mom. Let Skyler know I'm coming." She wiped her hands over her face and stood up, then held her hand out for me.

I got up, and Mara trapped me in a large, warm hug. "I love you."

"Me too," I whispered. "I love you too." For once, her hug didn't bother me.

TWENTY-TWO
♥
IT'S ALL FUN
AND GAMES UNTIL ...

Wednesday before prom, the news was all over the place. Not only was everyone talking about Harrison being arrested for hitting Skyler's dad, but they'd heard that Zane's dad was selling his car. Rumor had it that Loni met Zane's little brother and broke the news to him that she'd been secretly dating Zane. Apparently, Zed had promised to keep the secret, since he thought she was hot. He even went so far as to invite Loni over to the house, pretending to be the one going out with her so she and Zane could see each other. However, it all backfired when their dad overheard them talking about prom.

He flipped, and the rest is history.

The car was already on the dealership lot in Farmington. And Zane was forbidden to go to prom.

It was quite the excitement at school. Loni gave a ton of teary sniffles, and Zane kept his head down for the most of the day.

"Are you okay?" I asked him as we headed down the hallway after school.

"Meh." He shrugged. "I've had better days. You?"

I nudged him with my elbow. "I've had better *months*, but you know, at least I didn't lose the car I'd saved a ton of money for."

"Ouch."

"Sorry."

"Nah, it's okay. Just trying to decide if it was worth it or not."

I planted myself in front of him so he'd stop. "Standing up to your dad? Are you kidding me? Yes, it was completely worth it."

He tilted his head and gave me a funny look. "You know, when you put it that way..."

"Many people have lost way worse things standing up for their rights."

"I guess you live and you learn, don't you?"

"That's my theory." I grinned.

Someone bumped him from behind, and he took a step closer to me. Those hazel eyes went soft, and I could smell his cologne. "Do you know what I wish?"

The roar of kids leaving school sort of muffled into the background. "What?"

"I wish I could kiss you right now."

My brain skizzle-skerped to a stop. "Zane!"

"What? It's the truth."

"Gah." I pushed away and started walking again. "Why do you do that?"

"Tell the truth?" He was grinning.

"Try to make me all flustered. Stop it. You're totally

driving me nuts."

"Nope. I'm not."

"Yes, you are."

"Look." He glanced toward the door and then back at me. "If I was trying to make you all flustered, I'd actually kiss you. Right now, I'm behaving myself, and telling you it's what I *wish* I could do. See? There's a difference."

"Ha. Very little."

"Really?" It was his turn to stop in front of me. "Do you want me to show you the difference between kissing you and not kissing you? There is a difference. I promise."

Why was he such a dork? "Move. You're blocking the doors."

Zane laughed as he moved away and opened the door for me. "You know what I like about you most, Ellyn Dashwood?"

I started down the stairs. "That I can kick your trash?"

"Ha. I'd like to see you try!" He chuckled. "No, well— maybe. I like how you say it like it is."

I was just about to answer him when Skyler came jogging toward us. "Zane! Ellyn! Wait up."

We waited at the bottom of the stairs for him.

"Isn't that the music teacher?" Zane asked.

"Yeah, he's got a thing for my sister."

"Hi." Skyler smiled as he approached. He wasn't even out of breath. "You probably don't know me, Zane, but I've heard about you in school."

"Oh." Zane shifted his backpack as Skyler cleared his throat.

"I know this is kind of weird, but I'd like to help you out."

"You would?" Zane seemed totally confused.

"Yeah, I heard about what your dad did, and that's so not cool. I've still got the truck that I used in high school sitting in the garage at my parents' house. It's completely paid for and everything. I'd like you to take it. For free. As in, it's yours. It's sort of a piece, but it runs. And it's got a good engine—should last you a few years, at least."

"What? Are you kidding me?"

Skyler shook his head. "Nope. My dad was asking me last month if I had any plans to sell the thing, and I don't, so take it. Use it. I'd rather see it go to a good cause than rusting at home. Besides, now you can take your girl to prom like you wanted to."

"But what about your dad?" I asked him. "Couldn't you use the money to help with medical bills, or something?"

Skyler laughed. "Dad's insurance is completely covered by the school district. He's been there so many years, that's the least of our worries."

Zane looked more overwhelmed than I'd ever seen him before, completely at a loss for words. So I stepped in. "He says 'yes. Thank you—I really shouldn't—but I could use some wheels, so I won't overthink this too much. Maybe later I can work out a way to pay you back.'"

Skyler laughed. "Perfect. You're welcome to hitch a ride with me now, and I'll let you see her."

"I can't believe this is happening." Zane looked so adorably baffled.

"Just go." I nudged him. "And say thank you."

"Thank you!"

Skyler put his arm around Zane's shoulders. "Come on. You can thank me later after the shock has worn off."

I giggled as Zane allowed himself to get tugged away. "Bye!"

There. Now the world could right itself again.

I was so giddy, I almost starting skipping on my way home

from school, but I stopped myself just in time to remember that I wasn't always the most graceful person. I couldn't believe Skyler would do something like that for someone he didn't even know. Even in the midst of his own trials, he was thinking of others. But then again, seeing how Maralyn was starting to cheer up, he definitely had some magic.

Skyler's magic wasn't over just yet. On Friday, the night before prom, he had another trick up his sleeve. He and Maralyn had been spending every other night together, just talking about life—her grief about Dad and Skyler's worries—so it didn't surprise anyone when he came to the door that night.

However, when it included one charming kitten with a big ribbon around her neck, I began to wonder if something was up. "Here," he said as he handed the ball of fluff to Mara. "I thought you could use something soft to make you smile."

"Aww…" She melted. I melted. Katelyn melted. Even my mom—who hates cats—melted.

"She's so adorable." I stepped forward and rubbed a finger over the kitten's fluffy fur.

Maralyn rubbed her nose into the kitten's sweet little neck. "I love her so much." It was then that she noticed a small white piece of paper attached to the bow. "What's this?"

Skyler grinned. "You've got to see for yourself."

Mom held the kitten while Maralyn took off the note and read it. "You're inviting me to prom?" Her jaw dropped.

"Well, I'm assuming you already had the dress, and I didn't want you sitting here in the house feeling lonely, so I thought it was the only practical thing to do—invite myself to your prom."

"But will the school allow that?" Mom asked.

He shrugged. "Technically, they don't pay me anything, and I'm doing a huge favor for them, so I'm pretty sure no one is going to say anything. Especially since I already got the principal's approval." He looked back over at Maralyn. "So, what do you say?"

"Yes!" Mara laughed. "How fun. I'd love to go with you."

Skyler looked surprised. I didn't realize he'd been worried that she'd turn him down. "Really?"

"Of course!"

I was genuinely happy for her, and decided now probably wasn't the time to bring up that we'd sort of planned to go together. Even though it was grudgingly, I had begun to look forward to it. Or at least, to showing up in the green dress.

Anyway, it didn't matter. What mattered was that Maralyn was beginning to see what an amazing guy Skyler was. And she was happy again. And hopeful. She needed this—way more than I needed to be seen in a green dress.

I slowly stepped away as Mom, Katelyn, and Maralyn continued to coo over the sweet kitten. I shut my bedroom door and contemplated all the good things that were happening around me. Even though life was full of insane drama, there was a tiny glimmer of hope beginning to shine through.

And hope was good.

I walked over to the closet and opened the door. There was the dress. I had absolutely no intention of showing up at prom by myself. And as long as everyone stayed preoccupied with Maralyn's excitement, I wasn't going to bring it up at all. No one even needed to remember that I'd gotten a dress. I mean, I could wear it next year, right?

Zane had messaged me on Facebook the night before,

thanking me for the awesomeness that was Skyler's truck. He was positive I had something to do with it, but I didn't. I had no idea at all that Skyler even had a truck—which I was quick to explain.

I imagined Loni's joy in realizing she still got to go to prom, and that Zane wasn't being punished quite as much as his father wanted him to be.

Then this sort of numbness came over me. I went over to the pink chair and sat down, just processing everything. Hopefully, Mara would continue to blossom through Skyler's kindness, and hopefully, Zane's happiness continued to grow. I really had some incredible people in my life. I had so much to be thankful for. So very, very much.

And I hated prom. I did. I always have.

Still, I felt small for a selfish moment. Small, and a teeny bit forgotten. I took a deep breath and stood up. Time to focus on homework or something—anything but this.

The next day dawned all bright and cheery. Mara was a whirlwind of excitement and eagerness that everything be perfect. She spent hours on her hair and makeup, I even helped at one point, getting the curling iron to capture her ringlets perfectly before setting them with bobby pins. It was just so much quicker to help with the back than having her struggle to reach it all. By the time she was done, Skyler had arrived to take her out for dinner before prom began.

I helped her slip on her dress and then watched her twirl in front of the floor-length mirror. She looked amazing. "Beautiful!" It wasn't the pretty purple Cinderella one, but it was pink and elegant.

Mara smiled and gave me a hug. "Thank you for all your

help! I can't believe I actually have a date."

"He's so awesome, isn't he?"

"You know, I didn't think so at first, but yeah, he's pretty much amazing."

"Have a blast." I waited for her to remember me, to have some sort of regret at not going together so I could brush it aside and tell her it didn't matter, but she didn't. She spun around one more time and then rushed out the door toward a very happy Skyler.

The "ooh"s and "ahh"s from Katelyn and Mom were what Maralyn needed most.

After I heard Mom begin to take pictures, I shut my door. That odd numbness came over me again. I tried to make sense of it. It didn't matter. None of it did. This was exactly how I wished to be tonight—home alone, while Maralyn dazzled everyone at prom. This was my dream.

So why was I acting so silly all of a sudden? Two ridiculous tears found their way down my cheeks. In frustration, I wiped them away. This was so stupid. I took a deep breath and plopped down in front of the long mirror. All Maralyn's makeup was still scattered on the floor.

As I looked at myself, I reached over and began to apply the makeup the same way she had put it on me the other day. If I was going to stay home, there was no reason why I shouldn't look pretty doing it, right?

I had to steady my hands to put on the eyeliner—that was the hardest part. After about fifteen minutes or so, Maralyn's face stared back at me. I guess putting on makeup wasn't as hard as I thought it'd be.

I pulled my hair out of its messy bun and then brushed my long curls. Then I found a discarded headband full of crystals, like a tiara—probably something Mara had considered before choosing to do her hair a different way. I slipped it on my head, just past my bangs. It was really pretty.

Smiling, I realized I felt a bit better. I stood up and pulled out my dress, just to see what it would've looked like with the sparkly band on my head. I removed the plastic bag and pressed the dress up against me, holding out the long skirt. I loved how enchanting the soft layers were. I rocked from side to side to watch the skirt swish across my feet. When I caught my reflection in the mirror, I looked like a princess.

I couldn't remember a time when I looked and felt more beautiful. I glanced over at the dresser. The two tickets Mara had gotten for us were still there. Maybe, just maybe, it wouldn't be so bad if I showed up to prom after all. I didn't *have* to be with someone. I could go just to experience it and feel pretty and be there. I didn't have to be miserable just because I wasn't dancing. I determined my own experience, not anyone else.

I squared my shoulders, lifted my chin, and stared at the gorgeous girl before me. This was the girl my dad saw. This was the girl Maralyn and Zane and my mom saw. How was it that I'd never seen her before?

I think she'd been hiding way too long. I took a deep breath and then smiled, letting go of all that fear of rejection. I was holding myself back—no one but me. And it was time to show myself I was worth it too.

The dress glimmered in the mirror. I was just about to put it on when Mom called from the other side of the door. "Hey, Ellie, someone's here to see you."

TWENTY-THREE
♥
GOOD THINGS COME
TO THOSE WHO WAIT

"Coming!" Who was here? All at once, I panicked. I didn't want anyone else to know my plans just yet. I put the dress down on my bed and whipped off the headband. Then I grabbed a ponytail holder and put my hair up in a messy bun. Okay. I look normal-ish. Nothing could be done about the makeup, but oh, well.

When I opened the door, I was stunned to see a tuxedo-clad Zane holding a bouquet of white roses in his hand. "I come in peace." He grinned and stepped forward, handing me the flowers.

"But . . . how? Why? Aren't you supposed to be heading to prom about now?"

"Yep. I am." He pulled out two tickets. "Funny thing is, my date took one look at my new set of wheels and ran."

"What?" I couldn't believe what he was saying. "Loni isn't going to prom?"

"Oh, she's going all right. Seems she's been getting to know someone new these past few days and feels he's a better fit for her. Well, he and his nice Mustang, of course."

"Wait. What? Who?"

"His name is Zed. We've been known to play on the same team from time to time. And he's a couple of years younger than me, but she doesn't seem to mind."

"Oh, my gosh. Loni went to prom with your—"

"With my brother. Yes. It's true."

I didn't know whether to laugh or cry. "Are you kidding me?"

"Nope."

"I mean it. Are you kidding me right now?"

"No." He chuckled. "Is that all you're going to say?"

"Probably. It's about all that's coming out."

"I noticed." He was so good-looking, standing there in my living room, I could hardly breathe. "So I came here to ask this gorgeous genius I know to come to prom with me. I've only been falling for her for weeks now. I figured since I was free and all, it was time I did something about the irrational feelings I've been having."

"Irrational, huh?" I moved the flowers to one hand and stepped forward.

"Yes. It's bad. I get nervous when I'm around her, and I have a hard time focusing on what she's saying because I find myself wanting to kiss her more than I want to talk."

I blushed. "Are you kidding me?"

"And there she goes again, being loveable. I'm sure there's a cure for saying that all the time. Maybe we should find it."

"What do you mean?"

"I mean, I wonder if a kiss will help you not ask that

question again."

I was just barely hanging on. "I doubt it. I'm still in complete shock right now."

He moved until the tips of our toes were touching, and then he grinned down at me. "Your mom and sister have left the room. I think we can finally talk for real."

I laughed. "Haven't you been?" I'd totally forgotten about my mom and Katelyn. Not that it mattered—nothing did except for Zane.

"I know I don't deserve you," he whispered, his warm breath sending shivers across my cheek. "I know I'm a brat who treated his girlfriend badly because I was in love with you."

My breath caught in my throat. "You—you were?"

"Yes. I am."

"Are you kiddin—?"

He kissed me soft and slow and sweetly, and shut that question right up. "Did it work?" he asked as he pulled away.

My lips missed his the second he pulled away. I could hardly breathe—but it was a good feeling this time. I grinned. "I think so."

"Good. And for the record, I'm being serious."

He couldn't love me. It wasn't logical. I stepped back and shook my head—even though my heart was soaring. "Good grief. You didn't even know me. You still don't."

Zane tugged on my elbows and brought me close to him again. "You're wrong. I knew there was something unique about you the second we met. My heart started racing, and I felt this pull toward you. You were so amazing, I had to know more. I had to understand how your mind works, to talk with you for hours. I'd finally found a girl who understood me. I fell for you so hard that first day—I've never been such a fool like that before. Who leaves their car and walks a girl home?"

"Guys who are crazy."

"Guys who are falling in love."

My heart stopped. I honestly couldn't respond. He loved me. He loved me. He loved me! How was this possible?

"So, will you please come to prom with me? I don't know how I got so lucky to have my girlfriend dump me on the exact day I was wishing she would, but it happened. I don't care that she's with my brother—I hope they're happy. I only care that I can be with you."

"Well, ironically, I do have a dress."

"Good!"

This was even better than going alone. "And surprisingly, I do want to go."

"How about food? Are you hungry, too?"

I grinned. "I could eat something."

"Perfect. Now, how soon can you be ready?"

"About five minutes."

"Are you kidding me?" He laughed. "You are the perfect girl!"

"Now look who's asking that question." I bit my lip and told myself to calm down. Then I attempted my first real flirting. "Should I kiss you for saying it?"

"Are you kidding me?" he asked again.

I chuckled and pushed against him. "Go away. I have to get ready for prom!"

By the time I'd gotten dressed and fixed my hair again, Mom had her camera all ready. She was gushing with excitement that both of her girls were going to prom. She made us wait while she pulled apart the corsage Zane had gotten for Loni and replaced it with the new white roses he'd bought for me. Then, with the same floral tape, she took a couple of roses and created a boutonniere for him, too.

"There! Now you look like a real couple."

"Thank you, Mom." I gave her a hug, since she was getting all emotional. Then I gave Katelyn a hug too.

She whispered, "He's so cute!"

I chuckled and answered, "I know."

"Well, go and have fun!" Mom shooed us toward the door. "Katelyn and I are going to stay home and eat ice cream and watch chick flicks."

"Yep." Katelyn beamed. "We even got rocky road ice cream!"

"Well, we've been put in our place." Zane opened the door and walked me out to his chariot.

I started laughing the second I saw it and couldn't stop. It was one ugly beast. "That's awesome."

"Apparently, Skyler loved four-wheeling back in the day." The junky gray truck had a huge lift on it, large tires, and different-colored doors, hood, and tailgate. "Seems it's been through a lot, and the salvage yard has saved this baby more than once."

"No wonder why Loni wouldn't go with you." I'd never seen anything more ridiculously wonderful in my life. "I'm terrified of how awful the seats must be."

"Don't! I put down trash bags so you wouldn't get your dress dirty."

I was still laughing. "Shut it. How perfect."

"What?" He chuckled. "Don't you love my ingenuity?"

"You're the perfect guy for me."

The door creaked as he opened it. "I'm glad to hear it, m'lady. Your carriage awaits."

Giggling, it took three tries to finally get my foot up high enough to climb into the cab. Once inside, I straightened out my gown over the black plastic trash bags and then waited for him to bound up and start the engine. "This smells just like my grandpa's old truck."

"It probably *was* your grandpa's truck." He winked as he pushed on the clutch and revved the old engine, then threw the thing in reverse and backed out of the driveway.

It creaked and bounced, but it was fun.

"So, it's not as quiet as my other car, but I'm happy to have wheels."

I looked over at him and really searched that good-looking face. He'd definitely taken a step down by driving this thing, but he didn't care. There was something pretty wonderful about finding a guy who was grateful for what he had. Zane really wasn't after money, or popularity—he was his own guy. Hence the reason why he was turning down his dad's business. I needed him. I needed someone real and genuine, who actually saw me. I couldn't believe that guy was sitting next to me, dressed up, handsome as ever—and all mine.

We didn't have a lot of time, so Zane stopped by a burger place and we went through the drive-thru. We tucked napkins under our chins and ate in the parking lot as quickly as we could. Then we popped some gum in our mouths and made it to the Elks Lodge a few minutes before they closed the doors.

As we walked past some chattering couples in the decorated foyer and into the loud dance hall, we heard a few gasps and whispers, but it wasn't until we stepped onto the sparkling dance floor that the real stares began. I'd forgotten that Zane was a big deal, and how only just a couple of days ago, he'd had the whole campus talking about how he lost his car because he was dating Loni.

"Well, aren't you the one to get the gossip going?" I asked.

We stopped in the middle of the floor, and he placed his arms around my waist. "Believe me, the last thing they're talking about is me—it's all you."

I slipped my hands around his neck. "They probably think I'm Maralyn."

"Well, not for long, they won't." He spun me in a couple of quick turns.

"What does that mean?"

"You'll see." He grinned.

I loved him. I couldn't wait to get to know him more, but what I already knew, I craved. He was simply everything this heart of mine could imagine. "I don't know what you've got up your sleeve, but an hour ago, you didn't even know if I was coming with you or not."

"I know," he whispered in my ear. "But I still called in a favor anyway. Just to guarantee the school knew, even if we didn't show up."

I would've begun to feel a bit of apprehension, but I was too distracted by his arms around me to care much. "You're lucky I like you."

"You love me. Admit it."

"How would you know?"

He waggled his brows. "Oh, I know. I always know."

"Brat."

He suddenly dipped me low, and I shrieked as I clung to his arm. "I've gotcha." Slowly, he brought me back up, with those hazel eyes shining into mine. I had no idea life could be this happy. None.

"Forgive me for not having you break up with Loni

earlier."

"Oh, now you tell me."

"I didn't realize how this would feel."

"What?"

"Being with you." I looked away and then said, "We should've done this weeks ago."

"Yes, yes, we should have!"

TWENTY-FOUR
♥
ENCHANTING EVENING

I caught sight of Loni and Zed at one point during the night. She didn't seem too surprised to see me with Zane, but by the look on her face, I could tell she thought she'd snagged the better brother. She could have him. Gladly.

When Maralyn and Skyler danced by, they turned around and hung out with us the rest of the night. Skyler could really move! And with Mara's training and his skill, they cleared the floor a few times. No one watching them would ever doubt they were a couple.

"Are you having fun?" I asked her as we hurried to the ladies' room for a bit.

"Yes! Why didn't you tell me how cool Skyler was?"

"I'm pretty sure I did."

"I really like him. I didn't think I would like him this much—but every day I know him, I like him more." She glanced over her shoulder. "And what's with you and Zane? I thought he was going with Loni—at least, that's what one of my friends said yesterday."

"He was."

She paused for a moment as it all clicked into place. Then her face went pale. "How long have you known?"

"That they were together? Since we moved here. But it was a secret, so I couldn't tell anyone."

She took a step forward and then whipped around. "But I saw the way he looked at you. He was falling for you—I know he was."

"Yeah." I nodded.

"But he was already taken. And you didn't want to hurt her?"

"Yes."

She shook her head and then gave me a bear hug. "I'm so sorry I said all those things to you. You had this horrid secret and no one to tell it to, and I only gave you a hard time about not understanding what was happening to me."

I couldn't believe it. Maralyn actually got it. She understood what I'd been going through.

"Don't look so surprised." She sniffed. "I was a jerk to you, but that doesn't mean I wouldn't recognize it now."

"Well, thank you."

"Will you ever forgive me?"

"Of course. I don't even think about it."

"But I was stupid and rash, and I should've been more sensible, like you. I should've stopped and seen what I was doing and how awful I was behaving. You are and have always been the wise one."

I shook my head. "I think you give me way too much credit."

"And you're also the modest one, too." She grinned and looped her arm through mine. "Right. Let's head to the loo and then get back to our super-hot dates."

"Sounds good to me."

About an hour later, all Zane's hints began to make sense. The DJ stopped the dancing, and he began to announce the king and queen. When Zane's name was called for the king, the cheering was incredible, but then the DJ hushed everyone down. "Wait, wait. There's something I have to read here first. This was sent to me by the king himself a couple of hours ago. Apparently, Zane had a feeling he'd need this read tonight. He was right." The DJ cleared his throat, and Zane didn't go up on the stand. Instead, he looked right at me.

"I would like to dedicate my crown to the girl I love, Ellyn Dashwood. There is no other heart more honest and truly royal than hers. For that, I ask that you please give the crown to her so everyone can see who this incredible person is. I love you, Ellyn. My crown is yours."

"Holy—What just happened?" My mouth was gaping open in amazement. The place was roaring with excitement, and everyone was clapping, and really, I just wanted to hide.

"Go on. Get the crown."

"I'm not going up there! I could actually die. I'm serious—I could."

Zane took my hand and walked me up to the podium. Then he placed the crown on my head and stood me up in front of everyone. "See? It's not so bad, is it?"

They were clapping, but the girls were in awe. "I think you just won the record for best boyfriend ever," I hollered over the noise.

"Does that mean you're claiming me?" He smiled.

"This . . ." I pointed to the crown. "Has definitely proven that, whether I like it or not."

Thankfully, the song began. I ignored the queen—one of

Maralyn's dance team friends—and instead went right back into Zane's arms. "Thank you for my crown."

He bent down and kissed my nose and then my lips. "Thank you for loving me. I don't know what I'd be doing right now had you not moved into my town and into my heart."

"Meh. You'd have lived, I'm sure."

He gave me a very skeptical look. "No. Life before you wasn't living. It was just . . . there. *Now* I'm living. Now the whole world is mine."

"It always was. You just had to take it."

He kissed me then, long and wonderful and sweet. I didn't think I'd ever get used to the butterflies his kisses caused. There was no way this night could get any better. None at all.

I was so wrong.

About ten minutes later, the DJ stopped the music again, this time to make an announcement. "Skyler Brandon, your mom's been trying to get through to you. Check your cell phone. Your dad woke up from his coma. He's gonna make it!" The room roared to life, and Skyler actually had tears on his cheeks.

"Your mom says to get your butt up to the hospital and give him a hug. He can't wait to see you."

Skyler and Maralyn raced from the room, the crowd cheering for them.

Much later that night, after all the hoopla of prom was over and Zane was walking me, bare feet and all, up to my house, he wrapped an arm around my waist and asked, "So, was prom everything you thought it'd be?"

I tucked the crown under one elbow and dangled my

shoes from my fingers. "I don't know. It was fun, I guess. I'm not sure if I'd ever go again, but it was okay."

"And that is what makes you so much more amazing than anyone else in this town."

"Because I don't go crazy over prom?"

"Because you're all about the moment. Enjoying real things. You don't let your head get turned by nonsense. Because you're levelheaded and drama-free and just wonderful."

I didn't know about levelheaded or drama-free. It seemed like I'd had my fair share of drama the last few months, but I certainly wasn't going to disagree with the guy.

"You know what I love about you?" I asked as we reached the door.

He shook his head with that adorable grin of his. "I can't even imagine."

"Because you see me. You care about me. And you take time to care about those around you—beyond the norm. You care more about someone's soul than you do their acceptance. You're pretty much perfection."

"Well, how can a guy argue with that?" He kissed me again—right on our small, dingy, rented front porch, under the sparkly, starry night—for all of Bloomfield to see.

You know, when I lost my dad, I thought my world had truly ended. I had no idea what was in store. I couldn't have imagined that all those things he used to tell me—all those silly dreams—would come true. I'd almost given up on hope, love, and life.

But then, it took one kind person to see me. Someone to love and accept me for who I was. To encourage me to be myself and to show others that even though I was different, I was wonderful, too. I found beauty through the eyes of others.

And I found me by finally accepting the truth that had been spoken to me all those years, by letting the negative talk out and bringing in the joy and hope around me. Once that was achieved, everything else fell into place.

Dear Readers—

Because of you and your love of this series, I have decided to expand the Jane Austen Diaries to include three more books: *Sand & Sun, The Wilsons,* and *Queen Sydney.* These are based on Jane's lesser-known works, but I think you'll find the stories just as enjoyable. Thank you for your love and for taking this journey with me. You are all amazing!

Love,
Jenni James

ABOUT THE AUTHOR

Jenni James is the best-selling author of twenty-five books,
including series that are still in the works. She has written the
Jane Austen Diaries, the Jenni James Faerie Tale Collection,
Andy & Annie, and Revitalizing Jane, to name a few. When
she isn't writing and dreaming up even more books to write,
Jenni can be found nestled on the tops of the mountains in
a gorgeous little cottage. There, she has several chickens,
turkeys, fruit trees, and a garden.

Please follow her on Facebook: Author Jenni James
to keep up with all her latest works.

You can learn more about Jenni at her website:
www.authorjennijames.com
Visit Jenni's publisher, Trifecta Books, at:
www.trifectabooks.com

Made in the USA
Charleston, SC
09 December 2016